MAYA NICOLE

D1362191

ASCEND

CELESTIAL ACADEMY BOOK 1

Emily,
You don't need
wings to fly!
♡ Maya Nicole

Social Media

Join my Facebook group for release date updates
and teasers.
https://www.facebook.com/groups/mayanicoleauthor

Instagram @mayanicoleauthor

Twitter @MayaAuthor

Playlist

Don't You (Forget About Me) - Simple Minds
Runnin' With the Devil - Van Halen
Pray - Sam Smith ft. Logic
Hey Child - X Ambassadors
The Truth - James Arthur
Novocaine - Hidden Citizens
Baptize Me - X Ambassadors & Jacob Banks
Sucker - Jonas Brothers
Exit Music (For a Film) - Radiohead
River - Leon Bridges
Nothing Else Matters - Metallica

Author's Note

Ascend is a reverse harem romance. That means the main character will have a happily ever after with three or more men. This book also contains male/male romantic encounters, as well as several romantic encounters together as a group.

Some scenes may trigger some readers due to PTSD flashbacks, abduction, bullying, and a relationship with a teacher in a college academy setting.

Recommended for readers 18+ for adult content and language.

ick. Tick. Tick.

I stared down at the beige and gray flecked linoleum tiles as the sound of the seconds ticking by echoed in my ears. I ran a hand over my jean-clad thigh, smoothing a miniscule wrinkle.

Glancing at the clock, the red hand taunted me as it made its slow circle around for fifty-eight beats before hesitating and then clicking twice in quick succession as the minute hand moved forward. It was torture listening to it. It's like one day a clock-maker said, 'Hey! Let's make the loudest clock possible to put in schools!'

It seemed louder in here with the office staff quietly chatting, answering phone calls, and clicking away on their computers. They glanced up occasionally to check on me, to make sure I was still in the rather comfortable armchair situated outside Mr. Miller's closed office door. I itched to take my phone out of my backpack to check to see what people were saying on Twitter, but didn't dare pull it out in the office.

It was an office I was all too familiar with. It was a chair that might as well be engraved with my name. It was a well-known fact that the chairs in high school offices were specifically designed to create a false sense of comfort before the guillotine came crashing down. That was how I felt, as if my head was about to be lopped off *A Tale of Two Cities* style.

Mr. Miller and I saw each other more often than I'd care to admit. He told me he didn't like seeing me in his office so much. That he saw me more than he saw his own son, which I find to be a gross exaggeration. Last time I was here for disrupting class, he said that I was an adult now. That I needed to get my act together before I ended up in a different type of concrete building. A concrete building where they didn't care that my dad worked all the time and left me practically to my own devices.

My own devices put me near the bottom of the entire senior class and at the bottom of a discipline flowchart he referred to every time I was sent to him. I was a smart woman, even though my grades might not have reflected that. I knew what was coming. I was actually surprised it hadn't happened already. The flowchart dictated what action Mr. Miller had to take, no matter his sympathies towards me. He warned me every time I was suspended that my time was running out to turn myself around.

Maybe I would just get my GED. Would I even *pass* the GED test? I could get a job. Could I get a job without a GED?

My body jerked as a secretary slammed a file cabinet shut, the metal on metal echoing in the sterile environment of the hall. I let out a long breath of air and picked a piece of lint off my shirt with my bruised hand. It still stung, but the ice the nurse gave me helped. Too bad ice wouldn't help what was about to happen.

My last suspension was my last chance and now the glint of metal sat ready and waiting above my outstretched neck. They called my dad, even though I was eighteen now. I begged them to call my former caregiver like they did before my eighteenth birthday, but they refused. I was screwed.

My dad was a busy man with an important job, and the last time he came for something I'd done, his wrath was merciless and I was grounded for months. That was back when I was kicked out of the private school where they didn't dick around or put up with the same "juvenile delinquent" behavior as public schools did.

My friends always bitched about their parents and their rules. Their consequences. Well, I had them beat. My dad tortured souls for a living. Dealt their punishments. Condemned them to suffer in the fiery pits of hell.

Literally.

My eyes snapped up as I heard the front door of the office open. I couldn't see him from where I was sitting, but I felt him. The smallest whispers of discomfort spiraled up my spine and caused my shoulder blades to tingle with an itch I couldn't quite scratch. I slouched down slightly in the chair as his voice carried across the room and into the hall.

"I'm here for my daughter, Danica Deville." I shut my eyes as his smooth, yet slightly gravelly voice drew the attention of several of the office staff.

Whatever initial reactions they had to his demanding tone quickly vanished as they took in his tall, lithe frame, and his mesmerizing dark eyes. They sat up a little taller in their chairs and patted their hair to make sure it was in place.

The principal's secretary stood and fumbled with the latch on the swinging door that blocked the lobby from the back offices. "She's right through here, sir. If you could have a seat, Mr. Miller will be right with you," she said with a slight tremble in her voice.

My heart stuttered as my father came into view. He flashed a white smile at the secretary that crinkled the corners of his eyes and caused a small dimple in his left cheek. The secretary placed one of her trembling hands on her chest as if it would stop the fluttering of her heart. I covered my mouth with my hand, a smile threatening to escape at her display. It was hard not to laugh when he came into a room and put people under his spell.

My dad made his way towards me, his shiny brown shoes making a clicking noise on the floor, much like the ticking of the clock. Today he was wearing a brown three-piece suit, the color reminding me of a blonde coffee bean, with a navy tie tucked neatly into the suit vest. He sat down in the chair next to me, the scent of firewood and cinnamon hitting my nose.

"Danica."

I bit my lip and shifted in my seat. He probably would have much rather been attending to the souls down in hell than in a stuffy school office dealing with my transgressions.

"I'm sorry." The words came out as a breath. I only half meant the words. I was sorry he was here, not for what I had done. I was also sorry for turning out to be a failure of epic proportions.

I clasped my hands in my lap and kept my eyes focused on them. I could feel my father's eyes burning into the side of my head. I knew when he looked away because the slight warmth his gaze caused dissipated.

The principal's door opened and I lifted my eyes to meet those of my best friend, Ava. Her blue eyes were red from crying. She looked past me at my father and her eyes went wide before snapping back to mine. She gave me a very slow shake of her head before exiting the office. If she had a tail, it would have been tucked between her legs.

Ava was caught in the crossfires, dragged into the middle of something I was keeping her out of. She had a scholarship to a top university to protect. Her headshake was all that was needed to let me know that the guillotine was locked and loaded.

"Mr. Deville. If you and Danica could step into my office." Mr. Miller stood by his open office door and gestured inside.

I entered in front of my dad, as he stopped and shook Mr. Miller's hand in a firm handshake that I'm sure left my principal feeling uneasy, but he didn't show it as he took his place behind his desk.

The room was silent, the only sound the faint office noises on the other side of the closed door. During my three and a half years at Montecito High, the principal's office had remained the same, except for the man behind the desk. He looked tired now.

I reached out and straightened Mr. Miller's name plate. He steepled his fingers just under his nose and then let out a long sigh.

"Mr. Deville, I'm sorry to call you in like this. I know you're a very busy man."

"Please, call me Michael," he replied, flashing another award-winning grin that didn't reach his eyes. He was not happy to be here.

"Michael," Mr. Miller said, testing the name out. By the way his eyes narrowed the tiniest bit, it was clear he didn't think my father's name was actually Michael. It was like he could sense the wrongness of it on his tongue.

It's not like my dad could go around calling himself Lucifer Deville. It would raise too many eyebrows and garner too much attention. He decided his name would be Michael when he was here. It was akin to giving the angel the middle finger.

I was sure the angels were well aware that Lucifer visited this place, but left him alone unless he gave them reason not to. I would have thought him using the name Michael would piss some of the angels off, especially Michael, but perhaps it wasn't worth their time or effort.

"As you know, we have tried many interventions to help Danica succeed, and she has already been granted an additional chance by the expulsion review board. Given she continues to disregard rules, her failing grades in almost all of her courses, and her assault of a young man this morning, the district is going through with expelling her."

"I see." My dad was no longer smiling. Instead, his eyes were on me again, sending a sharp slap of heat to my head. It didn't hurt, but was uncomfortable.

At that moment I didn't know if failing out of senior year and being expelled simultaneously was rock bottom, or the fire that was smoldering next to me was. I braved another glance in his direction, keeping my chin down, and saw the pupils of his eyes dilate inside the smoky gray of his irises. He was assessing me, no doubt thinking of how he was going to punish his half human, half devil daughter.

At least torture was out of the question, not that he'd ever do that. We weren't entirely sure I was immortal anyway. I was uncharted territory. Something that shouldn't even be possible. Yet here I was. Lucifer's daughter.

He released me from his stare and looked back at Mr. Miller. "She assaulted someone? That is out of character, even for her."

"Well, as you know, she has been showing increasingly troublesome behavior over the past several years."

Out of the corner of my eye, I caught my dad clenching his jaw ever so slightly. No, he didn't know because I didn't tell him and my caregiver was too nervous around him to tell him. He knew about the expulsion hearing; it was mandatory since a joint was found in my locker, but he hadn't even attended that.

"This morning, one of the boys she has been in verbal altercations with before approached Danica and handed her a flier to his church. She punched him and broke his nose." He paused. "The boy's family has decided not to press charges, since she will no longer be attending school here."

"You punched a boy because he gave you a flier for a church?" Lucifer may have sounded calm, but his voice was a slightly lower timbre that caused goosebumps on my arms.

I gritted my teeth and swallowed the bile that had slowly worked its way into my throat. My father may very well be the devil, but never once had I heard him speak ill of the big man upstairs. At least, not in front of me. I couldn't tell him the real reason John had offered me that flier, he'd kill him.

I shrugged. Nothing I could say at this point would help. Ava telling Mr. Miller that John had done more than just hand me a church flier certainly didn't get me out of being expelled. John was the golden boy of the school. No adult would believe a juvenile delinquent like me. Especially if I told them the church was not a church but a front for drug dealing.

Lucifer cleared his throat and turned his gaze back to Mr. Miller, who was watching our exchange with piqued curiosity. My dad had this detached manner about him, where he didn't show his emotions, even when the situation called for it. He'd probably act the same if we were sitting discussing my college prospects. Which by the way, were non-existent, especially now.

"I'll just need you to sign this document. One of our school resource officers is cleaning out her locker and will bring her personal belongings." Mr. Miller slid a paper across the desk and my dad took a pen out of the inner breast pocket of his blazer.

He never signed anything with other people's pens. He said it was too risky, that there was always a potential for blood shed. As if a high school principal would put some kind of spell or something on a pen. He took a moment to skim the page and then signed his name in flowing cursive that was much too pretty to be that of Satan himself. He slid the paper over to me and offered me his pen.

I let out a long sigh and signed my name under his. I slouched in my chair as the paper was slid back across the desk and Mr. Miller signed his name. It was all too simple, sealing my fate with a flourish of a pen. No senior prom. No senior week. No graduation. No future.

Mr. Miller left the office to make copies of the document, leaving me alone with my dad.

"Sit up. You did this of your own accord, now deal with it." To an outsider, his words would have sounded passive, almost bored. But his eyes were glossy and his face too stoic.

I sat up and glanced over as he looked at his watch. Today he was sporting his Louis Moinet Meteoris; it had a piece of a meteorite from Mars in it. Seemed a little extravagant to me, but it was one of his favorites. He had a thing for fancy watches and there was no better place to keep them safe than his lair in hell. Sometimes I felt he took better care of his watches than he did his own flesh and blood.

Once Mr. Miller returned with copies and a bag of random junk I had in my locker, we left the office and walked towards the student parking lot.

"Keys." Lucifer held out his hand as I dug in the front pocket of my backpack for them. Tears pricked at the corners of my eyes as I handed them over.

We got into my black Nissan GT-R and I threw my bag in the backseat. Lucifer was peeling out of the parking lot before I could even get my seatbelt buckled.

"Jesus! Don't hurt my baby!" I gripped onto the door handle as he drifted around a corner.

He laughed and took his foot off the gas. "Yours? Last time I checked, the pink slip was in my name. And you can't tell me you don't drive it like this. You are my daughter, after all."

I might be his daughter, but I was at least a semi-sane driver. He drove like a bat out of hell.

The rest of the ten-minute drive to our house was quiet, the only sounds in the car the faint sound of the radio that was practically turned all the way down. He wasn't a fan of popular music or small talk. When we got to the gates leading up the long drive to the house, my stomach clenched.

He pulled into the garage, still silent, his jaw set, and I followed him into the kitchen where he turned on his espresso machine. I sat at the island

and watched as he made himself a cup of espresso. He then grabbed me a Diet Dr. Pepper out of the refrigerator and slid it across the smooth surface of the island.

I knew he was going to ream me after he finished his drink, but despite that, I had missed him. He visited once a week for dinner with me, but the rest of the time he spent reigning over hell and his army of demons. FaceTime and texting just weren't the same as having him around.

When I was little, I used to wonder where he was all the time. The first time I realized he was different was when I was about six. Surprisingly, I had convinced him to go to my elementary school harvest festival. It was warm, but he still chose to wear a suit. He always wore a suit and I had never seen him wear anything else.

It was there, in the middle of the carnival when he was buying me ice cream, that I realized he was different than the other parents. The other parents didn't seem to think it was weird he was wearing an expensive suit while they were in jeans and T-shirts. In fact, they had looked at him as if he was the most beautiful man they had laid eyes on. Even the men.

It's not that he *looked* different than a human, but there was just something about him and his presence that sent emotions soaring. Especially if a person had done something that was of question-able morals. Most of the time he blocked me from having to feel this aspect of himself, but I could tell he was letting just a little bit of his fear inducing spell, or whatever it was, leak out.

I took a long gulp of my drink and put the can on the counter, popping the tab off and fiddling with it. I watched as he rinsed his cup and put it in the dishwasher.

"What's your plan?" He leaned against the counter opposite the island, crossing his legs at the ankles.

I continued to fiddle with the tab, spinning it on the counter. "I guess get a job. Any job openings in hell?" A laugh left my lips and died a silent death as he stared at me. There was no way he was going to let me live or work in hell. No. That would be impossible.

I had only been to hell once. For five minutes. Five minutes of pain.

"What about college? Get your GED and then enroll in some classes."

Here I was having a conversation with the devil about taking college courses as if everything was normal. Everything was definitely not normal.

"I don't like school. You know that. Maybe I can help your demons with some of the jobs they do here." I looked at him hopefully.

"Absolutely not. You aren't meant to..." His voice trailed off and he stared past me and into the living room before running a hand over his face. "You're not meant for that life."

I cleared my throat. "You're the devil."

"That doesn't mean I want you to be. Your mother would skin me alive."

My chest felt tight and I grabbed my soda and took another drink. "My mother is dead."

He ran his hands over his tie, pulling it from his vest and loosening it around his neck before dropping his hands to his sides and clenching them open and closed a few times.

"A fact I'm very well aware of." He pulled his phone out of his pocket and swiped across the screen. "I've been thinking that maybe it's time I reach out to the others."

He rarely talked about them, but from what I could tell from the brief mentions of them, they weren't enemies, but they weren't friends either.

"What do you mean reach out to them?" I narrowed my eyes at him before following him into the living room as he pressed buttons.

He glanced up briefly from the screen before he held it up to his ear, the faint sound of the ring-back filling the quiet room. I plopped down in my seat on the couch and pulled a pillow into my lap, hugging it to my chest. He went to the window and opened the curtains to look out at the backyard.

When he started talking to whoever he had called, his grip tightened on his phone and his voice sounded like it was shaking slightly. I squeezed the pillow tighter.

After a few strings of bullshit small talk he got to

the point. "I have a daughter... I don't know how it happened... Yes, I'm sure she's mine... She doesn't have wings..." He finished his conversation and inhaled a sharp breath before slowly turning to face me with a tight smile on his face.

"Chamuel will be here in five minutes." He set his phone on the coffee table and sat on the edge of a chair. He straightened his tie and shoved it back in his vest.

I watched his movement before scooting over to the cushion at the end of the couch nearest him. "You invited an *angel* here to the house?" I shrugged out of my sweater, suddenly feeling hot, and ran my hand over my mouth. "Why would you do that?"

He shut his eyes before shaking his head as he spoke. "My blood hasn't changed Danica. That makes you half-angel. Maybe I've been wrong in keeping this from them. Especially since I can't be here all the time and your attraction to trouble."

I stood up, sending the pillow I was holding to the floor and crossed my arms over my chest. "So *now* you suddenly show interest in how much trouble I'm causing?"

He opened his mouth and then shut it. After clearing his throat, he said, "You're walking around punching people in the face. Who knows what else you've been doing. So, yes, I'm concerned."

I let out a laugh at the absurdity of the whole conversation. The devil was concerned that I had punched someone in the face. At what *I* was doing when he left me alone eighty percent of the time to be raised by nannies and caregivers.

"And where were you?"

He flinched at my words but didn't say anything before he stood and went back to stare out the window.

"Let me know once you and the angel decide my fate." I kicked the pillow out of my way and ran up to my bedroom, slamming the door shut behind me.

I really should have stayed downstairs.

Chapter Two

My inability to not act impulsively really got me into a pickle, and not just a slice of pickle on a hamburger, but a world record-sized gherkin of a pickle. Had I stayed downstairs, then maybe I could have at least argued with what Lucifer and Chamuel decided was best for me. Instead, I had given them all the power to make my life miserable.

Yes, I was of legal age. Yes, I could say no. But could I really? I had no family to speak of besides Lucifer, and independent living without a high school diploma in the Santa Barbara area was an impossibility. So pretty much, I was screwed.

I pulled the tape dispenser across the box and sealed it shut, the sound making my ears want to bleed. Maybe I could invent a quiet packing tape dispenser and not be shipped off to hell.

I had never had to pack my belongings before.

We had always lived in this house; well, I had, at least. I had kissed my first boy and lost my virginity here. I had gotten drunk and high here. All things that a father who was present shouldn't have allowed to happen.

I put together another box and dumped my underwear and bras into it before throwing a stack of tank tops and t-shirts on top. I really needed to pare down my collection; it was borderline excessive. Some people liked their shoes, I liked feeling sexy at all moments of the day by way of a lot of lace in every color under the sun. At least I'd have cute underwear underneath the hideous uniforms at the training school I was being shipped off to.

I hadn't even known there were schools for angels until Lucifer sat me down on the couch later that night and dropped the bomb on me. Los Angeles Celestial Academy, one of four academies for college-aged guardian angels. Located in the Angeles National Forest under special protective wards, it was where the top angels were sent to hone their angel knowledge and skills.

I was definitely not a top angel. I wasn't even sure I qualified as one given I had no wings and hadn't died. There were two ways to become an angel: being created or ascending upon death. Once a soul had ascended they were faced with a choice to remain in heaven or serve a greater cause and become a guardian angel on Earth.

I don't see how Chamuel thought sending me to

an academy to become some kind of savior was in mine or the world's best interest. What could I offer someone in their time of need? A toke from a joint I used to attempt to stay focused on my school work? Maybe a swig of vodka from a water bottle? It was doubtful my soul would even make it to heaven if I died. I wasn't bad per se, but I certainly wasn't good or angel material.

Besides having an extra class to study for my GED (which Lucifer was adamant about), I'd be subject to tortures such as Defensive Flight Techniques, The Portrayal of Angels in Modern Literature, Introduction to Demonology, and General World Studies. Shoot. Me. Now. I had barely even made it to trigonometry.

Ava entering my bedroom snapped me out of my pity party and I snatched my hot chocolate with extra whipped cream from her hands. There were most likely not any Starbucks where I was going unless I wanted to drive thirty minutes into the city.

"Are you sure you really have to go? You're eighteen, you could just get a job," Ava said flopping down in my desk chair and taking the straw out of her drink to lick the whip cream from it.

I sighed and dumped my jean drawer into another box, not caring that by doing so I was wasting space. I looked at Ava and wondered what she would think or say if she knew the truth about me, about Lucifer. She was so strait-laced it would probably rock her world. We were unlikely friends to say the least.

"You've met my dad, right? He doesn't care that I'm eighteen. What he says goes." I taped the box shut and grabbed a red Sharpie to write on it. "Plus, it's not like I can get a job that pays well without a GED."

Ava leaned forward to see what I had written and snorted a laugh. I couldn't wait to see the reaction of the angels as boxes labeled with dildos, bondage, and porn were carried down the hall.

"What is he, a mobster or something? Just tell him you aren't going and move out. I bet my parents would let you stay with us for a while." She stood and grabbed the Sharpie from me before adding the word 'hardcore' to the box labeled 'porn.'

"It's a little more complicated than that." I looked around my room, making sure I wasn't forgetting anything. "I think I'm all packed."

Ava put her arms around me. "Promise you won't forget about me."

"Don't *you* forget about me." The musical quality of my voice caused us to both belt out *Don't You (Forget About Me)* by Simple Minds a la *Breakfast Club*. It was a fitting song for us to sing considering I was about to endure the longest detention in the history of detentions.

∼

THE SUV that came to pick up my boxes was a pearlescent white monstrosity that screamed angel, and not just because two angels were driving it. The two men that were sent to pick up my boxes kept staring at me when they thought I wasn't looking, and not because they found me attractive. Although I'd like to think that maybe a small part of them did.

It also didn't help that I had every box labeled inappropriately. So inappropriately, that one of the men had stepped out into the hallway and made a call. Surely angels had sex and had senses of humor.

I followed behind the SUV for the almost two-hour drive from Montecito to Angeles National Forest. Had they seriously set up a school there because of the name? Hell, the school might have even been there before Los Angeles was even a city.

My stomach tightened as we drove on the two-lane highway and turned down a gravel road. Dirt and rocks hit the sides of my car and I flinched thinking of how tortured my car must be feeling. Black was the worst color for dust.

As we traveled down the dirt road, I felt rather than saw the shift in the air as we passed through the wards that hid the campus amongst the trees. As we came down a hill, it came into view and I couldn't help but let my mouth fall open.

There were ten massive brick buildings that spread out across a wide area with large swaths of grass and trees. I'd been entertaining the thought that it might look like Hogwarts, but it looked like something straight out of the English countryside. The grass was so green it felt out of place in the drought-stricken area. Maybe that was why Southern California was perpetually dry; the angels were stealing all the water.

I followed the SUV to a smaller brick building set off from the rest of the buildings and parked in an empty spot. There were only a few other cars, most being SUVs. I guess they didn't need cars here since they had wings and all that jazz. Even if I did have wings, I'd still want a car.

I slid out of my car just as a man walked out the door and walked over to us. I licked my lips as he approached. He was singlehandedly the most attractive male specimen I had ever laid eyes on. His dark brown hair was cut short and looked like he had run his fingers through it. His beard was close cut and well groomed. He looked muscular with wide shoulders and a narrowed waist under his blue Dodgers sweatshirt. I bet he had abs. Men with shoulders like that *always* had abs.

His brown eyes quickly took me in from head to toe before he met my eyes. I wondered what he was expecting when he was given the task of greeting me. I felt naked instead of having on a pair of skinny jeans and crop top that bared about an inch of my stomach. I should have put on a longer shirt.

No. No, I wouldn't change who I was just

because I was in the presence of angels. They were humans once; surely they had seen some skin.

"I would have taken you for an Angels fan, not the Dodgers." I smiled lightly and stood a little straighter.

His mouth turned up slightly before falling flat again, and he shoved his hands in the pockets of his jeans. "I'm Tobias Armstrong. I'll be your advisor and instructor for one of your courses."

His voice was... well you know how there's that phrase, voice of an angel? There's some truth to it. It made my breath catch and I cleared my throat, hoping he hadn't noticed. I took a step forward and reached out my hand.

"Danica Deville." Instead of taking my hand in a handshake, he shifted from one foot to the other before pulling a key and fob out of his pocket and holding it out over my outstretched hand.

A dull ache started building in my chest because, what the hell? Who doesn't shake someone's hand when offered? I turned my hand palm up and he dropped the keys into it. I stared at them in my open hand before I curled my fingers around them, my hand shaking ever so slightly.

I had known going to this school was going to be difficult given who I was, but after my interactions with the movers and now this guy, I wondered what the students were going to be like.

"This is the faculty and staff building. The dean felt it was better to have you here than in the student dorms." He offered no other explanation, and he didn't need to.

The ache spread like someone was sitting on my chest and my feet felt heavy. He turned and walked towards the door he had exited from. They were scared of me. Scared of what I might do to the other students here.

"Are you coming?" He glanced back at me with slightly raised eyebrows.

I nodded and plastered on a smile before following him. He scanned his own fob and we entered a large common room. I was immediately drawn to the large fireplace with chairs and couches angled towards it. I'd probably never get to enjoy it since I would be living with my teachers.

I groaned internally at the thought of being under their scrutiny at all times. I probably couldn't get away with smoking or sneaking out. Pasadena wasn't that far away, but any hopes of at least some-what enjoying this torture-fest were slowly dwin-dling away.

"Where is everyone?" I asked as we approached a large split staircase. There wasn't another person in sight; surprising since it was Sunday.

"Working." It didn't seem he was going to give me much more than that.

"Isn't Sunday supposed to be a day of rest? Hell, Chick-fil-a is closed but an angel school has people working?" I bit the inside of my cheek after the words left my mouth. He grunted but didn't respond. I was setting a really good first impression and probably digging my grave deeper.

I increased my pace to catch up to him so I wouldn't be tempted to watch his ass as we walked up the stairs. There was no denying that he was attractive. We went to the right and into a hallway that had several doors. The only sounds were our shoes on the hardwood floors. It was a ghost town.

We stopped at the last door and he moved out of the way so I could open the door. I was pleasantly surprised at the size of the room and the attached bathroom. They may have stuck me with the teachers and staff, but at least the room was decent enough. The furniture was white wood and included a full-sized bed, dresser, desk, futon, and a small kitchenette.

Tobias didn't move an inch from his spot near the opened door as I looked around and pulled the curtains open to let light in. I could see clear across campus to what looked like a football field.

"Does this work for you? Chamuel didn't really tell us what to expect."

I glanced over at him as he shifted from one foot to the other. He looked down the hall and then back at me. Clearly, I made him nervous.

"I'm a little disappointed with the size of the bed. I guess my days of orgies are over." I walked towards him and he quickly backed up into the hall, a slight pink tint creeping onto his cheeks just above his beard line.

"Uhh... well. You don't necessarily need a bed for that." Eyes wide and looking at the floor, his hand went to the back of his neck. He rubbed it before he brought it to his beard and then ran his hand through his hair.

I brushed past him and he leaned back slightly as my arm touched his shirt. It was subtle, the tiniest of movements, but it was enough to be noticeable. And painful. Was I really so revolting?

I took off down the hall without a word as the two angels tasked to moving me in walked by with narrowed glances. If Lucifer's goal was to punish me, well, this was doing the job.

ONCE I RETURNED to my room after sitting in my car while the SUV was unloaded, I looked through the binder left on the desk. There were so many rules and protocols. No smoking. No drinking. Lights out at eleven on weeknights. Blah. Blah. Blah. Who did these angels think they were, a military school for misfits?

I was eighteen years old and from what little I did know about this school, it was for college-aged angels. What could they possibly do if an angel broke a rule? Ground them?

I opened the window and let in the fresh air, suddenly feeling like the walls of the room were closing in on me. I still couldn't shake the hurt I had felt when Mr. Armstrong had visibly been repulsed by me. It's not like I had horns or even looked evil. Lucifer wasn't even evil.

Sure, he had a dark side. Anyone cast out of heaven would. If anything, the other angels should be grateful that he controlled the dark depths of hell so well. There hadn't been a major incident with demons in centuries.

Still at the window, my eyes were drawn to the football field in the distance where a group of angels were playing what looked like football but while flying through the air. I had never seen an angel all angelic like, with wings out. From my room they looked like giant winged birds.

I had asked Lucifer once if I could see his wings, but he refused. I wasn't even sure he still had wings. My knowledge of angels was limited to what I could get out of my father, which wasn't much.

My knowledge of demons was top notch. All of the time I spent grounded was spent reading books Lucifer provided.

I turned back to the binder, ignoring the rest of the sections that probably would have answered all my questions and pulled the campus map out. The campus itself was sprawling, but most of my classes were in a center building aptly named Uriel Hall.

My stomach growled as I located the dining hall on the map. I tucked the map and my phone in the back pocket of my jeans before throwing on my black leather jacket and heading out the door.

There were no signs of any staff members as I made my way out of the building.

The pathways weaving their way between buildings and around large grassy areas reminded me of old college campuses I had searched up on the internet. Despite my low GPA and nonexistent college plans, I still perused the websites since college was all Ava talked about.

This campus seemed out of place here in the mountains, hidden by magic I didn't yet understand. The brick building the dining hall and administrative offices were housed in loomed ahead of me. Five stories of aged brick and large windows rose into the sky with an angel statute perched at the top. I assumed it was Ariel, since the building was Ariel Hall. I bet they didn't have a Lucifer Hall here.

As I approached, the delicious aromas of food filled my nose. I could really go for a cheeseburger and Diet Dr. Pepper. I hoped angel food was no different than what humans ate. If they ate twigs and berries I was probably going to exist on cereal and frozen food. My room did have a kitchenette, but I could basically only cook ramen, and even then I managed to mess it up somehow.

I was almost to the small set of stone steps leading into the building when a group of seven angels landed in front of me by the door. I stopped in my tracks and stared slack-jawed at their expansive white wings. They spanned five or six feet on each side of their torsos. Somehow they managed not to bump into each other. One of the boys had wings that almost appeared silver in the fading light of the evening. They folded them back behind themselves and they seemed to disappear as I blinked.

I was considering how to get around their group as some of the boys pushed and shoved each other, when one of the girls in the group gasped as she made eye contact with me. She nudged the girl next to her and they started whispering in a completely obvious way. The five boys they were with continued to rough house and throw a football around as the two girls walked towards me.

Maybe they wouldn't know who I was. Who was I kidding? They knew *exactly* who I was. Every student on this campus probably knew Lucifer's flesh and blood was going to be attending. Maybe they had even gotten a warning notice to be on high alert.

"You must be the new girl we've heard so much about. I'm Delilah and this is Abby." A tall blond introduced herself and the other girl but neither made any move to get closer than a few feet away from me.

Both girls were gorgeous and had glowing skin and hair that looked like it belonged in a shampoo commercial. They held themselves like their shit didn't stink and appraised me by giving me the once over.

I smiled, my face feeling tight under the forced movement. "Danica. Are you all first years?"

Abby looked me up and down with raised eyebrows and pursed lips. "She looks normal. I was expecting her to be scary."

The girls laughed and I went to move around them to find the path blocked by the five male angels that had finally realized what was going on. Great, more attention.

"Well, what's this? The antichrist in the flesh!" One of the angels sneered and crossed his arms over his chest.

My fake smile quickly faded as I stared at the five male angels in front of me. They were all striking, and stood stoically with matching frowns on their faces.

"Can you move, please?" I really wanted to lash out at their commentary, but had to be better than that. They were expecting me to do something. Typically I would, but that was how I got into this whole situation in the first place.

"Or what? You'll unleash your demons to make us?" They all laughed like it was the funniest thing in the world.

I shrugged, deciding my words weren't worth wasting on them, and walked onto the grass to get around them. Their laughter faded as I entered into the dining commons. Heads immediately turned to check out where the laughter had come from in the brief moment the door had been opened.

I made my way to the food line that was similar to the dining commons I had seen on a field trip to UC Santa Barbara. A field trip that was wasted on me since I was not college material. I piled my plate with food and filled a cup with Diet Dr. Pepper before scanning the room for a place to sit.

I decided to sit in the corner at the end of a long table that was already occupied at one end. Right as I was about to sit down, a girl grabbed my arm, causing some of my drink to slosh out of the side of my cup.

"Don't sit there. The Divine 7 sit there. Come sit with us." She gestured to a round table somewhat in the middle of the room.

I stifled a groan. Middle of the room meant center of attention, which I already seemed to be. Eyes followed me as I walked and several students rose a little, trying to look at what was on my tray. What did they think I ate? I guess I couldn't blame them since I had the same question about them.

Once I sat down, I let out a sigh of relief and took a drink. Three sets of curious eyes watched me as I slowly put my cup back down.

"I'm Danica. Thanks for saving me?" I didn't mean for it to come out as a question but based on my warm reception at this school so far, I wasn't sure what this group's motives were.

"Oh, we saved you all right. I'm Brooklyn, by the way. Class III," the girl who had invited me to the table said.

"Ethan, Class II."

"Cora, Class II."

"What do you mean by class? Your year?" I took a bite of the pasta with chicken I had picked. It was surprisingly good, for you know, angel food.

"Class just specifies how we came to be angels. Class I are created by The Man himself, Class II died before they were age twelve, Class III died after twelve and are deemed pure enough to serve," Ethan explained. "Did your advisor not tell you what Class you were?"

"No." I spun my fork around my noodles, creating a very impressive bite that was almost picture worthy. "I think he was scared of me so I didn't get too many details about things here."

My three eating companions all looked at each other before going back to their own dinners. My shoulders were just starting to relax when the group from outside started to file past with their food.

"It eats real food! Holy shit, man." One of the guys nudged the guy next to him and they both stared openly as I took a bite.

I narrowed my eyes slightly and then started chewing my food with my mouth open. If they wanted to stare, I'd at least give them something to look at. Cora laughed as the two boys took off towards the back corner with disgust on their faces. I watched as all seven of the group from outside sat where I had first tried to sit. That was a close call.

"Why are they called the Divine 7? They don't

seem very divine." I put my fork down and took a bite out of the chocolate chip cookie I had grabbed for dessert. It seemed like a good time to have my cookie after enduring their bullshit.

"*They* call themselves the Divine 7 because they have the highest divinity rankings. Of course, that doesn't really take into consideration how shitty they might act on the sly. The two girls are the worst. Oliver and Levi aren't that horrible, but they also don't put a stop to anything. Oliver is the only Class I angel at any of the academies. We're still trying to figure out why he's here. They renumbered the class system this year since he is the first since the original archangels." Brooklyn looked over her shoulder at the table. "Oliver is the one examining his bread, and Levi is next to him."

I glanced briefly in that direction and Levi was staring at me, which he quickly tried to hide by looking away. Oliver really was examining his bread, which he sniffed before taking a bite. It wasn't a normal look and sniff, like a regular person might do. It was as if he had never seen it before in his life. I tilted my head slightly, trying to figure that one out.

"Can I ask you a question?" Ethan looked directly at me and was immediately nudged in the side by Brooklyn who then gave him a very annoyed look. I appreciated that at least Brooklyn seemed to somewhat understand what I was going through.

"Sure. I don't mind questions from people who

are nice to me." I finished the last bite of my cookie and braced myself for the questions I knew were going to come. I didn't mind as long as they were in good faith.

Ethan leaned forward on his forearms so our conversation couldn't be heard at the other tables. I had no clue if angels had supersonic hearing. I guess I also had a lot of questions to ask them.

"Did you actually like, *live* in hell?" I barely caught his question over the noise in the dining room. At least he was being discreet.

I couldn't help it, I laughed. "No I didn't. I went for maybe five minutes once before getting violently ill. I'm half human. I assume I'd get just as sick going to heaven."

Cora let out a relieved breath and Brooklyn just stared at me. If eyes could actually bug out of heads, Ethan's would have.

"So you lived with your mom, who's... human?"

"My mom died during childbirth so my dad hired caregivers. I lived right outside of Santa Barbara in Montecito my entire life."

"So you don't actually see... *him*?" Ethan was elbowed again by Brooklyn.

"He's not like Voldemort. You can say Lucifer and he won't suddenly appear and torture you." I laughed. The table next to us looked over at the mention of Lucifer's name. I hadn't spoken quietly enough. I lowered my voice enough so that only the three across from me could hear. "He comes for dinner once a week and we text and FaceTime all the time."

"Cell phones work in hell?" Cora had been quiet up until now. She seemed to be processing everything I had said.

I nodded. I used to wonder about how technology worked in another plane of existence. My dad told me it was magic. I wasn't entirely sure that explanation was accurate, but honestly, I don't think I wanted to know how the internet and cell service worked there.

Brooklyn changed the topic of conversation after that and we discussed our class schedules. I had two classes with her, one with Cora, and one with Ethan. I also learned that I'd only have to deal with Oliver and Levi in classes because the other five were second or third-year students with different classes. I left the dining room feeling hopeful that maybe this new school wouldn't be so bad after all.

Chapter Three

$\mathcal{I}$ woke up to the sounds of birds chirping somewhere outside my cracked-open window. It was the beginning of February, so it was a little chilly, but not having a window open made me feel claustrophobic. Plus, I liked piling the blankets on. It made me feel cozy and relaxed.

I went to the generously sized closet and looked longingly at the clothes I used to wear to school. Jeans, T-shirts, hoodies. Instead of having freedom of choice here at the lovely Academy of Asshole Angels, I had to wear a uniform. It was so cliché I wanted to vomit.

I pulled a uniform out and threw it on the bed before going to my box of underwear and bras I had yet to put in a drawer. I wanted to Marie Kondo the shit out of my drawers, but hadn't gotten around to it yet. What I was sure of was that every piece of lingerie I owned sparked joy within me and would not be going anywhere.

I dumped the box and found a matching set of red lace boy shorts and a bra. I considered putting the pile back in the box, but it really was my best intention to organize and fold them later. After putting them on, I eyed the uniform laying haphazardly across the bed. Thick white wool skirt with silver and navy-blue trim, white button up, blue blazer with silver crest on breast pocket.

First off, a man must have decided on a white skirt. I'd have to strongly consider getting a pair of those period panties as an extra precaution. Secondly, it looked like something a captain of a yacht might wear. I was experiencing serious FML in that moment, but at least the uniform was thick enough that I didn't have to wear boring undergarments.

I let out a curse as I picked up the shirt and jacket, realizing the back had two slits with about an inch of overlapping fabric, no doubt for angel wings to pop through. After putting on the sailor attire, I grabbed a Diet Dr. Pepper and a granola bar. One of the perks of being in the teacher building was a small kitchenette which had a half-sized fridge, sink, and two electric burners. Not that I'd use it much, but who knows, maybe I'd give cooking a shot.

I popped the top on my soda and took a long gulp as I went into the bathroom. Yes, I had an addiction to Diet Dr. Pepper. Some people liked their coffee, I liked my red and white can of crisp goodness.

I brushed out my brown hair and pulled it back into a loose ponytail at the base of my neck before putting on my makeup. I toned it back much more than usual, skipping the black eyeliner and fake eyelashes.

I grabbed my bag and was out the door with plenty of time to spare. I had to walk to class, unlike my winged peers, although I noticed a lot were walking as I approached Uriel Hall.

This was going to be tough. I was not only starting midyear, having missed the entire first semester, but three weeks of the current semester had already passed. Not going to lie, school was tough for me. It would have taken a miracle for me to graduate with Ds and Cs had I not been expelled. Most likely I would have been retaking a few classes in summer school.

It's not that I didn't *want* to do well in school, but I found it hard to concentrate. In high school, the teachers didn't seem to care. There were meetings. There was testing. They never blamed me, but medicine wasn't an option because it didn't work. Different seating didn't work. Videos and audio recordings of the class didn't work. The only thing that helped, even if just a little, was marijuana. Too bad it was still illegal for my age in California. Not that it had stopped me from getting my hands on any before, but then again that had led to me being scouted by a drug conglomerate.

I entered the building and made my way up two flights of stairs to room 306. Introduction to Demonology. I was actually excited, it being in my wheelhouse and all. Having some prior knowledge on the subject made me feel a little more confident as I pulled open the door.

Once inside the classroom I was immediately disappointed there were tables with two chairs at each. I hated partners. Well, really they hated me. It was a fairly large classroom with multiple tiers of tables curving in a crescent shape, much like a typical university. I looked to the front of the room and in the corner behind the teacher's desk sat Tobias Armstrong. *Great.* I was sure this class wouldn't be biased at all.

I walked over to the desk and stood by it while he typed something on his laptop. I cleared my throat and he looked up. His expression was hard to read. The day before he had recoiled and been annoyed with my presence, it seemed. Now, he had his teacher face on.

"Is there assigned seating?" Because God forbid I sit in someone's seat and taint it with my evil.

"Good morning, Danica." He went back to typing on his computer.

Yeah, maybe I should have greeted him. My elementary teachers always used to make us greet each other daily, but this wasn't elementary school anymore. Why did I need to say good morning to someone that looked at me like I was a piece of dog shit on the bottom of his shoe?

"Why don't you take a seat in the front row." He stopped typing and handed me a small stack with a book and folder.

I grabbed it from him rather roughly and sat off to the side, near the wall. I flipped through the book first. It was a run of the mill text book. Was there ever a class that didn't use a textbook? The teacher's job was to teach not force me to read chapters from an overly wordy book.

I flipped open the folder and found several pages of notes dated over the last three weeks. There was also a syllabus and list of assignments. Two had a line drawn through them with 'excused' written next to them. Thank goodness for small miracles. If I had to make up three weeks' worth of reading and assignments I'd lose it. Or I just wouldn't do it.

I took my spiral notebook and my pouch of Flair pens out of my bag and flipped the notebook open. I started at the corner of the page and started drawing a vine around the perimeter. Class must have started while I was doodling because the next thing I knew, Mr. Armstrong was tapping on the table in front of me. I looked up and met his gaze with raised eyebrows.

"You might want to take notes, Ms. Deville." I hated when teachers used students' last names.

I heard a few sniggers from behind me at the mention of my last name and watched as Mr. Armstrong narrowed his eyes in their direction before walking back to the center of the room. He smoothed down the front of his blue dress shirt and cleared his throat.

"In your reading last week, you should have read about Corpus Unguis demons. Who can tell me what physical features this demon has?" Mr. Armstrong went back to his desk and labeled a diagram that was being projected on the front board with the words 'physical features'.

I quickly flipped to the index of the book he had given me and found the page the Corpus Unguis demon was on. Skimming the page, I sighed. There were so many details that were incorrect or just flat out missing. That particular demon was complex and having half a page devoted to it was like having only a chapter about the Civil War in a history textbook. The angels' version of demon history was watered down just like a typical high school textbook.

A student near the middle of the room was called on and I turned slightly in my seat. Several sets of eyes stared back at me as I glanced around the room. None of my new friends were in this class. I did spot Oliver but quickly turned around before he could notice I had looked his way.

No one sat next to me.

Figures.

At least I'd have a seat for my bag.

Wasn't that the worst feeling in the world? Walking into a classroom and having no one sit next to you? I tried not to let it bother me, but it was becoming blatantly obvious I was the pariah of the school. I had been here less than twenty-four hours.

"A Corpus Unguis has five small heads with long tongues that have razor like protrusions on the ends. It has thick, almost clear skin that is impenetrable."

"Very nice. Now, why does this species have that type of exoskeleton?" He wrote down what the student said and turned back to the class.

Another student was called on. "It eats the fingernails from its victims."

I watched as he wrote on his notes. I raised my hand.

"Yes, Danica?" Oh, thank fuck he was using my first name. "Something to add?"

"It actually only has one head with five mouths. Its head is shaped like a hammerhead shark. I can see how it could be confused as having five heads though. Plus it doesn't eat the fingernails. It pries them off, chews them up, then spreads the substance over its armor to strengthen it. It actually has a serpent like body which is exposed in a few places."

The room was so silent I could hear my own heartbeat thudding in my chest. Fuck. Now I was *that* student.

"Why the fingernails?" I turned to see Oliver looking at me. "How do we kill it?"

"Usually it steps in when the soul has done something that warrants nonuse of their hands. An eye for an eye type of situation. To kill it..." I bit my lip. I wasn't sure how happy Lucifer would be if I divulged how. "I'm not sure how."

"Oh, I'm pretty sure you know how. Sounds like you are well acquainted with them. Your last boyfriend was probably a Corpus Unguis." At Oliver's words the class exploded into laughter.

"Enough!" Mr. Armstrong stood from his desk and stood in the front center of the room, rubbing his hands along his short beard. "Mr. Morgan, that will be five points off your divinity score."

"But, Mr. Armstrong, she's-" He protested before being cut off.

"I don't care what your reason is. I won't tolerate bullying in this classroom. If anything we should be grateful we have someone who is knowledgeable about something we hopefully will never encounter."

The rest of the class I continued my flowering vines and wrote down, instead of volunteering, the errors in the book. I could see how so many demons were misrepresented. They were all confined to hell and it's not like Lucifer had written the textbook. I'd have to let Mr. Armstrong borrow the book I had on demons. It would blow his mind.

Once class ended, I ripped my notes out of my

notebook and set them on his desk as I left the classroom.

∾

BESIDES THE HUSHED whispers and the occasional use of the word devil, I made it out of Uriel Hall and across the quad area to the gymnasium. I didn't love or hate gym class, but this class was Defensive and Offensive Flight Techniques. It was gym on crack.

There was one big problem.

I didn't have wings.

I made my way to the locker rooms and found Brooklyn already in her workout clothes. She greeted me and I quickly changed. Luckily there was no dress code for PE, so I threw on leggings and a tank top.

"How was your first class?" Brooklyn and her friends were the only ones so far to not throw hate my way, which was a relief. At least I had a few people on my side, or at the very least, in neutral territory.

She seemed to be on the quiet, shy side and reminded me a tad of Ava. She was shorter than me and had a head full of luscious curls that she wore in a sloppy bun on the top of her head.

"Oliver had five points taken away because he made some comment about the fingernail demon being my boyfriend. It's like we're in junior high." I shrugged like it was no big deal and I steered us towards the teacher, who looked awfully young to be teaching. "There's a student teaching?"

"Coach Ferguson? He's a Class II. He's about twenty-five in angel years."

I stopped in my tracks and grabbed her arm. "Run that by me again."

"He died when he was ten, drowned in a river. He's been an angel for twenty-five years, so he is thirty-five in human years, if that helps. Angels stop maturing in their early twenties. If they are older when they die they just stay that way, like Mr. Armstrong. All the really old Class IIIs go to a different academy."

"How'd he die?" I didn't know if that was a rude question, but if I was going to be asked if I had a pet hellhound or if I had horns, then any of my questions were fair game.

She shrugged. "Coach Ferguson told us his story the first day of school. Mr. Armstrong doesn't share much about his time before he became an angel. But I think I heard him say he was twenty-seven when he died."

We waited behind a student already talking to the coach. His eyes widened slightly when he saw me, but he finished his conversation before turning to me.

"Danica Deville, is it?"

I nodded in reply.

When he started to turn away, I cleared my throat. "Sir, I don't have, uh... I don't have wings."

A hush fell around the gymnasium. I hadn't even realized everyone was watching me so intently. This room sure did echo too.

"What do you mean you don't have wings? They let you in here without wings? How can you fly with no wings? This is an academy to be a guardian angel!" I was so tempted to roll my eyes at his stupid questions. Had I been back at my old school, I would have, and then I would have promptly been kicked out of class.

"Flap my arms really hard?" I raised my eyebrows and smiled. He didn't seem amused.

"You are an angel, right? What class are you?"

Crap, crap, crap. I had forgotten to find that little important piece of information out. I had meant to ask Mr. Armstrong.

Brooklyn, sensing my anxiety, stepped forward a little. "Sir, she is half angel. I don't think they have a classification for her yet. Maybe today I can prac-tice hand-to-hand combat with her since she missed first semester?"

"Good thinking, Russo." He gave me one last look before turning his back to me.

We made our way over to an area off the main gym. I had tried karate when I was younger and hated it. It was too controlled. What I really wanted was to learn how to throw down on the fly. I already knew how to throw a good punch at the nose though.

"Thanks. You deserve ten points for that," I said as we approached the door.

I heard footsteps behind us and turned to see Levi and two other boys. I turned back towards Brooklyn and nearly collided with her stopped body at the entrance to the area we were headed.

I heard laughter and my stomach clenched. Brooklyn spun around and glared at the three boys holding their stomachs in laughter. I stepped into the room where training dummies were spread at regular intervals and mats lined the floors. Taped to the dummy's heads were pictures of Lucifer.

Except it wasn't Lucifer. It was a red monster with a contorted face, horns, and red eyes. I went to each one and ripped the paper off. I didn't hear what Brooklyn said to them because my ears had done the strange, fuzzy ringing that happens when I get really pissed off, but the boys seemed to be laughing even harder. I walked over to them and stepped too close for comfort, because their laughing immediately stopped and they backed up a step.

"Maybe I should summon my father here to show you what he *really* looks like. And trust me, you don't want to see him when he's pissed off." The boys paled at my words and backed up another foot.

They didn't need to know that Lucifer didn't

have a demon form, or a different face. That's actually what made him so terrifying. He looked almost normal. The almost being that he had a penchant for fancy-ass suits and exuberant watches all while permeating hearts and souls with fear.

I wadded up the photos and threw them at Levi who jumped back to avoid their touch. I only wished I had the ability to throw fire balls. I turned on my heel and went back into the room with Brooklyn.

"That was... epic."

I gave her a tight smile but it was forced. I didn't want to use Lucifer as a threat, but these angels weren't leaving me with any other choice.

The rest of my classes and lunch passed without incident. Word had spread that I had threatened Levi and his two friends.

Good. Let them be scared.

At least if they were scared of me they would stop being assholes.

Chapter Four

Tobias

*T*his semester was really shaping up to be a shit-show of a semester. Just last week, the dean had called me into her office to meet with her and Chamuel. They told me I would be the advisor of Lucifer's daughter.

Lucifer's daughter.

I still couldn't quite wrap my head around that one. Angels weren't fertile. How the hell did Lucifer get a human pregnant? Had he used dark magic? Demon blood?

Chamuel didn't seem to know, nor did he care. He was all about peace and love. I'm not exactly sure what his thought process was behind allowing her to come to the most prestigious of all the celestial academies. We had standards here and after looking at her rather thick cumulative folder from her *human* education, she was far below what we would ever allow.

Besides lackluster grades that resulted in her frequenting summer school, she had a discipline record a mile long. A few suspensions with a day here, three days there. It painted a picture of a troubled young woman.

Pot in locker.

Defiance.

Disruption.

Assault.

Did Chamuel truly think we could fix this girl? She might have angel blood in her, but she certainly wasn't angelic. Maybe he was losing his touch because this place was definitely not the place for a half-blood angel that didn't even have wings.

On Sunday, when she had arrived, I had actually been surprised that she looked normal. A little better than normal. I guess I expected her to be goth or something. I wouldn't say angels ran around in skin tight pants that showed the sharp curve between their ass and hamstrings or crop tops that bared a flat stomach begging to be touched.

As she walked towards me that first day, I had known I was in trouble with this... woman. She stirred something deep within me that I hadn't even felt when I was human. It repulsed me. She repulsed me. Not because of who she was, but because I was the adult in this situation and she was, well, she was my student.

At least that's what I kept trying to tell myself.

Walking back to my room, I found myself thinking about her. She was already being bullied for who she was. Oliver might be top of the class, but his behavior was completely out of line and I don't think he was even aware how out of line he was. We had the other Divine 7 to thank for that.

They were supposed to be guiding him. Instead they were corrupting him. I wanted to intervene, but there were explicit orders from upstairs that he was to find his own path. Things probably weren't going to end well for him.

Even the other instructors were out of line. At lunch, Trey Ferguson had done nothing but complain about the half-breed in his class. She had no wings. She had an attitude. I couldn't argue with him there, she certainly had that.

Then there was Patricia Fisher, the Portrayal of Angels and Demons in Modern Literature instructor. She had docked Danica ten points she didn't even have because the girl had made a comment about her dad not being red. I hadn't docked her points for speaking out in *my* class.

I entered the common room of my building and nodded politely at the other staff members lounging on the soft leather sofas. Normally, I'd join them, but I wanted to work on updating our files on demons after the new information I learned today. Danica Deville might not be our ideal student, but she knew things we didn't.

Turning right at the top of the stairs, I stopped in my tracks as Danica stood outside her door and was wiggling to pull pants on under her skirt. A flash of red caught my eye but her gaze snapped to mine and I looked away.

What the hell was she doing changing in the hall?

And were those feathers on the ground?

Trailing out her door to where she was standing was a small trail of white feathers. Had she gotten her wings? If she had, then I needed to get her to the infirmary because that much shedding wasn't typical.

"Oh, hi, Mr. Armstrong." She zipped up her pants and stared at me as I started walking down the hall to my door.

She was at the end of the hall, I was in the middle. I stopped at my door but then turned to look at her before speaking.

"May I ask what you're doing?"

Now that I was closer I could see a few feathers in her brown hair and red blotches under her eyes, as if she'd been crying. My chest constricted at the sight and I felt the unwavering desire to step closer to her. To wrap her in my arms.

"Come and see for yourself. I'm just going to change my shirt in the stairwell." Her normal confident vibrato was absent from her voice as she spoke. I watched as she opened the door to the stairwell and slipped inside.

I peeked into her room but then moved to stand in the doorway, taking in the sight.

White down feathers lay all over the room. Everything, and I mean everything, had feathers on it. Her bed. Her dresser drawers that were pulled out. Her desk. Her bathroom.

My eyes went to the open window and I cursed under my breath. I hadn't thought to tell her to keep her window shut and locked, but how was I to know someone would do something so cruel?

I moved out of the way as she came out of the stairwell with a black tank top on that had a picture of the devil and the words "I'm horny" on it. I felt her eyes land on my quirked lips as I stared at her chest.

"So, yeah." She crossed her arms over her chest, which only made my focus on her breasts worse because it pushed them up. They'd probably fit perfectly in my hands.

No. No they wouldn't.

I looked down the hall, away from her. "I can call the custodian to come and clean this up."

"No! I... just let me take care of it." Her voice cracked and that made me ache to reach out and touch her.

To touch her, just like I had wanted to on Sunday.

God, how I had wanted to touch her.

"I'll get us some supplies to clean this up."

I went to the supply closet, which was right

across from her room, and grabbed black trash bags, brooms, and dust pans. I was a shitty advisor. I should have shown her around yesterday. Instead, I had run for the hills because she made my dick twitch.

We worked in silence for a few minutes before I let out a frustrated grunt and threw the broom down. "Who the fuck did this?"

I hadn't been that angry out in the hall, but now that we were trying to clean up the feathers, I was furious. Down feathers were the most annoying of all feathers. They stuck to everything and were so fluffy it was hard to pick them up, even with a broom and dustpan.

"I think it's pretty obvious angels did it, don't you?" She threw her broom down too, but with much less force than I had, and went to her refrigerator. "The assholes better not have put feathers in here."

She let out a puff of air as she opened the door and there were no feathers. Once the door was open, several drifted to the inside of the door at the bottom.

"Want a soda or water?" She took out a Diet Dr. Pepper and a bottle of water and held them out to me.

I grabbed the water and she looked relieved I hadn't taken the soda. I tilted my head a bit to the side and took her in as she popped the top and drank half the can in one go. She could have been a spokesmodel in a commercial with how sexy she looked drinking it.

"Why are you helping me?" she asked before putting her can on the counter and grabbing a bowl out of the cupboard.

She reached down and scooped up a bowl of feathers. Her face cracked into a grin at her ingenuity.

"Why would I not help you?" I started scooping feathers again.

"You're a dick."

I wasn't expecting that, that was for sure.

I paused mid scoop and looked up at her looking down at me. "What do you mean?"

"You think I'm repulsive. You all do." She spoke in an even tone that didn't give away any emotion. Either she was strong as fuck or had already come to terms with how the others felt about her.

"I don't think that. What gave you that impression?" My chest felt a little tight. Had I given her that idea? If she only knew how completely untrue her words were.

"The way you talk to me, look at me, flinch away when I get close." She lowered to her knees and continued scooping. "I would have at least expected the teachers to be more accepting."

I remained quiet. What was I going to tell her anyway? That the looks I gave her were more of an outward expression of the disgust I felt towards myself for getting a hard on for her? That when she got close to me I wanted to move away so I didn't do something stupid?

I couldn't tell her any of that.

Sure she was eighteen and of age, but I was her teacher.

Plus, I was old. Like died when I was twenty-seven during World War II old.

She let out a frustrated sigh and sat down in the feathers.

"How do angels get their wings?" Her hands lowered to the feathers beside her and she gathered them in her hands and watched the feathers drift down as she released them.

I continued to work and stopped near the dresser. "Well, there's a few ways..."

I struggled to find my words at the sight of her panties and bras laying in a heap on the floor. They were covered with feathers, but it was pretty obvious she liked lace. So much lace.

I turned quickly and moved away, hoping she wouldn't notice. She did.

"I'm lucky they didn't do anything to those, otherwise I'd have to go commando."

The thought of her without panties under that white skirt of hers made my dick twitch and start to harden. *Shit.*

"So, wings. Well, some are born with them. Class I, like Oliver Morgan. Class II usually get them immediately upon entering heaven. The rest of us have to go through a vetting process to make sure we are worthy."

"Lucifer didn't exactly explain all this stuff to me." She glanced up at me before she turned her attention back to playing with the feathers at her sides.

I hoped the way I was holding the trash bag was covering up my growing erection because I still couldn't get the image of her in that skirt with no panties out of my mind. Or how I'd love to bend her over my desk and-

What the heck was happening to me?

"I guess the easiest way to explain it is a person must have more light in their past than darkness. If there's more darkness they are sent to hell. If we are deemed worthy, then we're given tasks or jobs to increase the light. It might be as simple as singing in the choir for a year or maybe a series of selfless acts."

"You mean like a blow job? If that isn't a selfless act, I don't know what is." She laughed as she looked at me, a tinge of pink touching her cheeks. I felt all the blood drain from my face and straight down, making my erection throb.

She stood then and walked towards me and my breath caught in my throat. She reached her hand towards my face, and as much as I wanted to pull away, I stood still. Her pinky finger lightly touched my bottom lip as she plucked a feather off my chin with her thumb and forefinger.

I was headed down a dark path.

Not that angels couldn't have sex.

Sex wasn't the issue here.

She was a forbidden fruit, one that if I took a bite of I would surely be damned.

"You have a feather too." The words sounded stupid coming from my mouth, but they were out there and I reached towards her hair and brushed it off.

She pulled her bottom lip between her teeth and her eyes dropped to where I had just been holding the trash bag. The trash bag that I had dropped to brush the feather out of her hair. Her eyes met mine and I was certain that I wasn't alone in my sudden desire. It hit me like a lightning bolt.

I dropped the dust pan and brought my other hand up to cup her cheek. A warm sensation ran up my arm and to the center of my chest. My wings tingled in response.

"Shit." She backed away and turned away from me. "Sometimes I don't have a filter or boundaries. I'm sorry."

"Let me touch you again." I heard my words but they didn't sound like my own. My voice had lowered slightly. I felt a need swirling inside of me. I wanted to touch her. I needed to touch her.

"As much as I want you to, Mr.-"

"Tobias," I interrupted. I already felt skeevy enough as it was. Calling me Mr. Armstrong would only make it worse.

"Okay then, Tobias. I... okay."

I stepped behind her and picked a few feathers off her tank top, my hands shaking in the process. I ran a finger across her shoulder and felt her shiver with my touch. This was such a bad idea. Did she even really want me to touch her or was she just letting me because she felt she didn't have a choice?

"Tell me if you want me to stop."

I trailed my index finger down her arm before dragging it slowly back up. My body was thrumming with an energy I had never felt before. Even as a human I had never felt like this, and certainly not as an angel. Sexual pleasure was always slightly dulled, but not now. Not with her.

"I don't want you to stop," she breathed as my hand fell away from her.

Fuck it. For once in my life I was going to let myself lose control, consequences be damned. I lowered my mouth to her shoulder and kissed it lightly, drawing a sigh from her. I gently moved her hair out of the way and kissed my way to the base of her neck. It was taking so much self-control not to spin her around and capture her lips.

My hand went back to caressing her arm as I dragged my tongue from her neck to the strap of her tank top, which I grabbed in my teeth and pulled down over her shoulder. She let out a moan as I sucked her skin and planted kisses over the goose-bumped flesh. She tasted like heaven. If heaven had a taste.

My other hand threaded through her hair and pulled her head to the side to bare her neck to me. She whimpered as I lightly scraped my teeth over the spot just below her ear before sucking her earlobe between my lips. I don't know how I had gone from completely level-headed and professional to horned up and out of my mind.

My hands went to her waist and I struggled not to devour her whole. I had never wanted a woman so bad in my life and as she shivered and moaned with my touch and my kisses, I knew she had to be feeling the same.

My hand moved to her breasts, fitting perfectly in my hands as I kneaded them through her clothing. She turned her head and our lips met, a groan escaping before I let my tongue explore hers. I pressed against her back, letting her feel my erection against her ass. She pressed back against me before turning and grabbing my hair, bringing me closer, as if we could get any closer.

We were moving towards the bed. We were moving so damn slow towards it. She pulled me down with her, our lips never breaking contact, even when feathers floated around us. I settled between her legs so perfectly that I was anxious to get her out of her jeans to see just how well we fit together.

My hands pushed her tank up over her breasts and I pulled away to look. Her chest moved up and down as her lungs caught up with what we had just done. I traced my finger in a circle on her smooth stomach before trailing it up to her red-lace clad breasts.

I met her eyes and smiled. "No white?" I joked before lowering my mouth to the waist line of her jeans. She moaned as I licked the skin right above where her jeans touched. Her skin tasted like roses and what reminded me of licorice.

"What if I wanted you to wear white panties for me, or maybe no panties at all?" I glanced up at her again; desire was written all over her face.

I dragged my lips up her belly and kissed under her bra as I reached behind her and unclasped it. A sigh left her as she sat up and took off her tank. She grabbed the straps of her bra and slowly moved it down her arms to reveal her peaked nipples. I ran the back of my hand along the outside of her breast and she shivered. My thumb gently brushed over her nipple, causing her back to arch, bringing her closer to me.

"No more teasing. I want you to fuck me before I explode," she growled before grabbing a hand full of my hair and pushing my mouth to her breast.

If there was any doubt about her innocence or unwillingness, it quickly vanished.

I sucked and nipped at her puckered nipples as I unbuttoned her pants and pushed my hand between her legs. The lace between her legs was soaked through with her arousal. And I wanted to taste it. I wanted to taste all of her.

"You're so fucking wet," I murmured against her breast.

She moaned as I ran my finger up and down her hot, wet slit before pulling my hand out enough to slide back down into her panties. My fingers slid over a small patch of hair before my index finger dipped between her folds, her hips rising to encourage me further. Our lips met again in a forceful kiss.

Her hands slid down my back and cupped my ass cheeks. I took her bottom lip in my teeth as I plunged two of my fingers into her pussy. There was no turning back now; I was all in with where this was headed.

"Tobias, please." I wasn't sure if she wanted more from my hand, my mouth, or my dick inside of her.

"Tell me what you want, baby. There's no rush." My thumb found her clit and worked it in circles.

Her hands slipped around to my belt buckle and she fumbled with it as she dealt with the plea-sure I was bringing her. I used my free hand to help her and undid my slacks. Her hands slipped inside and found my bare cock, ready and waiting for her.

"I need this inside of me." She grabbed the base of my cock and began to work her hand at the same pace as I was moving my fingers.

I let out a groan before pulling my hand out of her pants and pulling her to her feet. I ripped back the quilt on her bed, sending feathers flying, but at least now we wouldn't get them in our ass cracks.

"Do we need protection? I have an implant, but..." She tilted her head back slightly to look at me, her cheeks flushed with heat.

How on God's green Earth did I let it get this far? Far enough that we were discussing using a condom, which she had no clue we didn't even need because angels were infertile.

Only now I was questioning that because how else had *she* happened? She must have read the hesitation on my face because she backed up a step.

"Unless you don't want to. I know it all happened a little fast." She bit her lip and started to pull her pants back up.

I was completely fucking this up. I felt like this was my first time, that awkward moment when you have to stop to fumble with the condom because putting a condom on a dick was way different than putting it on a banana.

"We don't need condoms."

Before I could mess up further, I pulled her back towards me and kissed her. I pushed down her jeans and panties and took off my pants. We sank to the bed and I put the tip of my cock against her opening.

Her phone rang and her face suddenly changed from sweet anticipation to annoyance. I pushed inside of her and we both sighed in satisfaction. What felt like lightning bolts shot through my dick and up between my shoulder blades. My wings ached to come out, but that might have ruined it for her.

Her phone rang again and she threw an arm over her eyes and let out a moan. Not a moan of pleasure, but a moan of frustration. I listened closer and heard the song, *Runnin' With the Devil* by Van Halen.

Crap. Her dad was calling.

Did he know?

Oh, sweet baby Jesus, did the devil know that I was currently buried balls deep inside his little girl?

I pulled out and rolled over next to her, both of us panting. My dick was still hard, but now I was slightly scared that he was going to show up and kick my ass. Or probably sic a Corpus Unguis demon on me since I had my hands all over her.

The phone rang a third time and she finally jumped up and went to her backpack to dig it out of the front pocket.

"For fuck's sake, *Lucifer*. What the hell is it?" she snapped into the phone.

I sat up abruptly, surprised she'd talk to him like that. Wasn't she scared of him? I mean, he controlled demons that chewed on fingernails like a cow chews on cud. I shuddered and felt my erection start to deflate. I didn't want it to, it's just now I was thinking about having my fingernails ripped off for touching her.

She rolled her eyes as she listened to her dad, Lucifer. The devil.

"Everything's fine. Great actually. Well, except for the name calling, oh, and the feathers covering my room. But I've made some friends." She looked at me and winked.

It gave me a little relief, that wink, but not enough to salvage the moment. Maybe that was a good thing; this was rather spur of the moment. I don't do spur of the moment. I should have asked her out for coffee or to dinner.

She listened to him talk again. "I appreciate your concern, but I have it handled... No, I won't punch anyone in the nose. I promise... You're way too overprotective... Love you too, bye."

She hung up and walked back over to the bed, sitting on the side, her back to me.

"Kind of a mood killer, isn't it?" She looked over her shoulder at me and down at my limp dick. "It's like he sensed a sin was about to be committed."

"What do you mean he sensed a sin?" I stood, panic flaring in my gut.

The last thing I needed was to piss off Lucifer, or any of the archangels, and end up without my wings. I saw what that did to a man and it wasn't pretty.

"It was a joke. We should finish cleaning this up. Maybe try to find one of those shop vacuums to use." She didn't sound like she wanted to finish cleaning it up but stood and went into the bath-room, shutting the door partway.

I heard the sink water, so I grabbed my pants, shook them out and slid them back on. I grabbed her clothing off the floor and shook them off the best I could. My heart was beating wildly as I grabbed her red lace panties. I looked back at the cracked bathroom door to make sure she wasn't looking and shoved them in my pocket. I left my shirt untucked to hide the fact there was something there.

When she came back out she looked for a few moments for them but then just grabbed another pair from her pile. How had we so quickly gone from zero to sixty? I was feeling whiplash and I was pretty sure I wanted it again.

Chapter Five

Danica

I hated when time seemed to slow infinitely when you were impatiently awaiting the weekend. It slowed even more when you had to deal with assholes and the fiery gaze of a particular teacher.

My encounter at the beginning of the week with Tobias was only that. An encounter. Sure, I had felt something beyond anything I had felt with a simple touch before, but I barely knew him. He barely knew me. It was not beyond my often-impulsive self to recognize that starting something with a teacher, my advisor nonetheless, was playing with fire.

And I'd probably be the one who got burned.

All week I had done my best to avoid him in the hall. It's not that I didn't want him, because I did. Every time I saw him my skin ached for him to touch it, but my mind was on other things. Like why the Divine 7 thought it was their duty to torture me.

On Tuesday before Demonology had started, Oliver very loudly announced that he was in desperate need of new pillows and asked for recommendations. Tobias looked murderous most of class, but did nothing, at least from what I could tell.

Then on Wednesday at lunch, Abby, Julian, and Levi walked by the table and dumped a plate of deviled eggs on me. Where they had even gotten them was beyond me since there had been none available when I went through the lunch line. I had wanted to retaliate but then Lucifer's warning echoed in my head.

The one he gave when he interrupted the pleasure train to an orgasm. The way Tobias had been touching me, kissing me. *Le-sigh*. Damn him to hell for calling.

Every time they said or did something, his voice echoed in my head. "Danica, don't get yourself kicked out of this school. This is your last chance." I wasn't sure what he meant by 'last chance' but I *really* didn't want to find out. There was only so far you could push the devil, and I think I had met my life quota ten-fold.

Thursday was freaking fantastic, and I should have known that it was the calm before the storm. The storm being my last class, which just happened to be independent study in the library. It was my least favorite class because I was studying for my

GED, which meant I had to focus. My focus was even worse because all I could think about was Tobias.

When he had touched me it was like fireworks had gone off in my body. No one had ever made me feel like that before. He worshipped my body, and despite barely knowing him, I felt some weird comfort being near him.

I was just finishing up a lesson on the computer when I heard something behind me. I hadn't even heard the library door open, so they had to have already been inside. Before I could even register the sensation to flee, a black bag was yanked over my head and I was jerked out of my chair by my arm.

Either the librarian was away or they had distracted her, because when I screamed, no one came. All there was, was laughter. Gleeful laughter. By now I knew that laughter well.

My hands were tied behind my back and then the bag was pulled up and a ball gag put in my mouth. I'd never be able to enjoy a ball gag now, thanks to those assholes.

Once they were gone, I managed to get the bag off my head by bending in half and shaking my head vigorously. The damn librarian was nowhere to be seen, so my only option was to wander into the hall.

I wish I hadn't.

I wish I had just stayed until the librarian came back.

At least some students in the hall looked at me in pity. Most laughed and took pictures with their phones. It would be spread around the school in a matter of minutes.

Someone finally untied my hands, and when I yanked the ball gag out of my mouth, well, no wonder it was so hilarious to everyone. It was in the shape of an apple.

I would have maybe even thought it was brilliant if they hadn't done it to me.

FRIDAY. Possibly the best day of the week. Well, besides Saturday and Sunday. Even school on Fridays didn't bother me too much since most teachers were always burnt out, which usually meant easy assignments or a video.

Teachers except Tobias Armstrong. A pop quiz on a Friday was not the way I had envisioned my day starting. I had half-expected a movie with demons. Tests and I didn't exactly see eye to eye. At least it was short-answer.

I found that short-answer was the best for me. I could embellish the hell out of my answers and usually at least get a few points. It's how I maintained my stellar 2.3 grade point average in high school.

When class ended, I pretended like I was

finishing up my quiz until the last student had exited and then handed it to Tobias.

"I won't be marked down for my descriptions being a little different than the book's, will I?" This was my main worry during the quiz, but I hadn't wanted to ask in front of everyone.

I was trying to lay low after the apple gag incident the afternoon before. I was going to be called Eve for weeks because of it. I didn't need everyone calling me an idiot too.

Tobias grabbed my paper and glanced over it. "No, but I will mark down for all these feather doodles you put everywhere." He smiled up at me, a glint in his eye.

Smiling was something he needed to do more often. It brought a light to his eyes that made me want to reach out and caress his cheek. He stared back down at my paper. "You've been avoiding me, Danica."

I ran my finger over the corner of the desk and then examined my nails to avoid his gaze. I felt it though. Felt it right between my legs.

"Come here." His voice was quietly commanding, which made my heart start to beat wildly. What if I refused and stayed where I was? It was tempting to defy him, but instead I moved around the side of the desk to stand near the drawers.

He grabbed my hand and pulled me closer. The same overwhelming need to be touched flared in my body, running up my arm, into my chest, to my core.

"Why have you been avoiding me?" He still had ahold of my hand so I couldn't escape.

"I haven't." I looked him square in the eyes, hoping he couldn't see what he was doing to me. I cleared my throat. "Is there anything I can do to make up for the lost points?"

"You can earn some extra credit." He let go of my hand and gripped my hip.

I was losing my resolve fast. This was why I had avoided him. Just his presence got me all worked up. It hadn't even been that long since I got laid, but I felt like it had been years. Monday's festivities didn't count.

"Get on the desk."

A jolt of excitement shot up through my toes and straight to my clit. We were in an unlocked classroom, but I wanted to get on the desk just to see what he was going to do. The thought of doing anything lascivious in a classroom at an angel school made me feel breathless. So, I slid my ass up onto the desk, my feet dangling off the side.

He rolled his chair away from his desk and slid it over in front of me, putting his hands on my knees. I took a sharp inhale of breath as he slid his hands up my bare legs, pushing them apart as he went. He let out a groan when his hands reached my panties and he slowly pulled them off, sticking them in his pocket.

My eyes narrowed on him and he smirked before he ran his tongue up my leg. I was already trembling and he hadn't even touched my pussy yet, but when he did I had to put the end of my jacket sleeve in my mouth to keep from crying out.

I thought his hands were brilliant, but his tongue was sinful. He pulled his mouth away and stood from the chair, kicking it back with his foot. I resisted the urge to touch my clit to finish the task he had abandoned.

"Is this part of my extra credit?"

He grabbed me around my waist, pulled me off the desk and bent me over so my chest was pressed into the stacks of papers on it. My body shook with anticipation as he lifted my skirt around my waist and ran his hand over my bare ass.

"Is your phone on silent?" he whispered in my ear, amusement in his voice, and pressed his erection against my ass.

I nodded, words alluding me in that moment, and he gripped my hip before thrusting into me, causing me to let a moan escape. I pushed his papers out of the way and brought my blazer-covered arm to my mouth to muffle my sounds as he thrust into me over and over again.

The last thing we needed was to be caught. I knew he didn't have a class, but the risk was there. A risk that sent a thrill through me. When I came, I came hard, sending Tobias to his own climax.

He rested against me while he caught his breath

then handed me a few tissues. I cleaned up and pulled my skirt down. I had just thrown the tissues away when the classroom door opened and Oliver Morgan, of all people, walked in.

He stopped in his tracks and his eyes went from me to Tobias, who was still buckling his belt, to the desk with papers shoved to one side, then back to me.

His face turned red as he went to where he had sat and picked up a notebook that was left on the desk. "Forgot my notebook."

Without giving us another look he walked out of the classroom, slamming the door behind him hard enough that I jumped in surprise.

"Shit. Fuck. Shit." I grabbed my bag and smoothed my skirt. "I'm late for PE."

That's not why I was freaked out. Now the whole school was going to know I was sleeping with a teacher. As if they didn't already have enough ammunition against me.

"Hey, don't freak out. Oliver isn't going to say anything." Tobias started straightening the papers on his desk. "And before you ask, yes, I'm sure. I know some things that he probably doesn't want everyone to know about."

My anxiety suddenly ebbed and my curiosity reared its ugly head. "Oh, really. Like what?"

He laughed and leaned towards me to give me a much too tame kiss. It was probably for the best since I was already fifteen minutes late to PE.

"Can't tell you." He finished straightening his papers and sat down in his chair. "Let me take you out to dinner tomorrow. Tonight I'm on call."

"Like a date?" My heart started beating a little faster and I crossed my arms over my chest, thinking he could see the change. He nodded. "Yeah, I'd like that."

"Good. I'll text you later. And Dani?" He grabbed my hand as I started to walk away. I turned and met his chocolate brown eyes. "Don't avoid me again."

I left the room on wobbly knees but managed to make it to PE with enough time left to be scowled at by Coach Ferguson.

~

AT LUNCH, I was nervous. Tobias's assurances did nothing to stop the pit of anxiety in my stomach. Plus, I had something planned to get a little sweet revenge. I hadn't been entirely sure I was even going to do it. That was until the apple gag was shoved in my mouth.

The deviled eggs I could deal with. Hell, even the feathers in my room was more of just an annoyance to get under my skin. But physically restraining me and putting their hands on me? That was where I drew the line between childish pranks and something more sinister.

"What are your plans for this weekend? There's

a party Saturday night we were going to go to." Cora interrupted my train of thought and I jerked my attention back to the lunch conversation. Angels had parties? Color me surprised.

"I have a dinner date Saturday night but if I get back in enough time I can meet up with you guys."

Cora and Brooklyn leaned forward in their seats.

"Do we know him or her?" Brooklyn looked like she was about to burst. She was all about the boys. She had never had a boyfriend, so I couldn't blame her for her curiosity.

Earlier in the week she had asked me about my love life, and when I told her I had slept with three men, she about died. Well, if she could have died again.

"No. It's our first date so I don't really have much to tell you besides he's hot." I imagined their faces if I told them the truth.

Honestly, I never had imagined myself with an older man, at least not one nine years older or however old he was in angel years. I couldn't help that I was attracted to him and wanted to know everything about him. He seemed to have no qualms about my age, at least from what I could tell. I decided to put my plan in motion instead of dwelling further on something that, at the end of the day, didn't bother me.

I reached down and grabbed the large manila envelope in my bag. When I was deciding on the vessel for the feathers, I had run through a million different scenarios. They were already going to be suspicious when I approached their table.

"What are you up to?" Ethan narrowed his eyes in my direction. Was I that obvious? "You have a shit-eating grin on your face."

"You'll see." I held the envelope between my knees and finished scarfing down my sandwich.

As if fate had determined this was an excellent idea, all seven angels waltzed through the dining room to their table with their trays. I had gone over my plan several times during my last class before lunch.

"I'll be right back."

I made my way to the Divine 7's table, and by the time I stood behind an empty chair next to Abby, the table had gone silent and six sets of eyes stared at me. All except Oliver.

"Eve, what do you want?" Delilah spat. Her eyes dropped to the envelope in my hand.

In the most irritatingly-sweet voice I possessed, I spoke. "I'm so happy you asked. Yesterday was a massive awakening for me." I shook my head as if I was disappointed in myself. "Until I saw myself with that apple in my mouth, I never thought about how our sins can affect those around us."

I looked at each of them before continuing. They at least weren't stopping me. "And all this time, for eighteen years, all I've done is sin, sin, sin. I thought who better to help me atone for my sins than the highest-ranking angels in this academy."

I held up the envelope, which was bulging. Their eyes followed it. "So I wrote down all of my sins on strips of paper and I figure if you can help me with one at a time then maybe, just maybe, I'll get my wings. The thought of going even one more day without them. It pains me." I put my other hand over my heart. Maybe a career in acting was in my future.

"You aren't serious, are you? You have that many sins?" Levi gestured to the envelope and had a look of amusement on his face.

"I don't even think I remembered all of them, honestly. Oh!" I made a noise of excitement. "I have one more I need to add that happened just today. I think maybe I should just tell you guys what I did and we can take care of it now."

At my words, Oliver's head snapped up and his eyes widened.

"Or even better!" I dropped the smile from my face. "How about I show you."

With my final words I started shaking the envelope down the length of the table as if it were a salt shaker. A few of the guys scooted back from the table, but most of the group sat stoically. Shocked. Flabbergasted. Probably already plotting my demise.

I sprinkled the last of the feathers on Oliver's and Levi's trays before dropping the envelope in front of Oliver. "And Oliver? I do hope your new pillows *satisfy* you."

I probably shouldn't have said that, but clearly he was uncomfortable with what he had seen this morning. If he had only walked in a few minutes before he would have seen a whole hell of a lot more.

I turned and walked back to my table, the entire dining area staring at me in silence. Some with scowls, some with admiration. They had heard it all. Hell, most of them probably knew about the feathers.

"Ms. Deville." Dean Whittaker seemed to appear out of nowhere and walked towards me with a deep frown on her face. "Please come with me."

Damn.

But it was totally worth it.

Chapter Six

*E*vidence. That was what Dean Whittaker said was lacking in my defense. I, on the other hand, had evidence against me. It's hard not to when you dump a giant envelope of feathers out on your enemies' food and the dean sees it happen with her very own eyes.

That was what they were now. My enemies.

Dean Whittaker said she wanted to give me a chance. A chance at what? A chance at sitting back and letting bully angels torment me? I kept my mouth shut, because unlike my former principal, the dean did not shoot the breeze or even care.

If she would have cared she wouldn't have brushed off my accusations of bullying like they were insignificant pieces of lint that landed on her shoulder. That was what she had called them. Accusations. The problems that plagued human schools seemed to plague celestial schools too.

Only it made it so much worse that they were angels.

Instead of even an ounce of sympathy for me—I had even showed her the pictures of the feathers and the apple gag—she took twenty-five divinity points from me and said she was assigning me a peer mentor because my points were at a critical level.

Critical my ass.

When points dropped too much, angels were sent to the high court for judgement on what action should be taken. Los Angeles Celestial Academy was the top academy for training angels to become guardians, but if a student wasn't showing promise they could be sent back to heaven or not be given any guardian tasks. Divinity points were the way they kept track. I didn't even have wings, so did points even apply to me? I didn't dare ask.

I left the administrative offices feeling deflated. It was rare my heart was so irrevocably twisted to the point it hurt to breathe. Not even when I was expelled, or that time the school resource officer threatened to throw me in a juvenile detention facility if I was ever found with pot again.

This was different. The very essence of who I was, was being attacked. Villainized. And for what? For being different? I honestly didn't even feel I was that different. Yes, I made mistakes, maybe even more than average, but did that make me evil? I didn't *feel* evil.

When I got back to my room, I pulled up Face-Time. It rang twice before Lucifer answered. I stared at the wall behind his desk which was covered in art depicting him. He got a kick out of it. To me it was just a reminder of how everyone saw my father and now how they saw me.

"Dani, just a second." His voice sounded far away, like he was on the other side of his office.

When he did appear, he was buttoning the top two buttons on a dress shirt. I briefly wondered if he had just gotten up or if he had been working. Lord knows why he would need to change his shirt after working.

"I'm leaving," I stated bluntly. Really no use in beating around the bush.

He sat in his chair and put laced fingers under his chin, searching my face. I was glad he couldn't interfere with my emotions through the computer screen.

"And where will you go? Back to Montecito? What will you do?"

I had been thinking about that question since he told me he was sending me to the Celestial Academy. "I have money. I'll just get a job at Starbucks or something, so I'm not bored."

"You hate the smell of coffee." His voice was neutral, which always made me leery of what he was thinking. "And what do you mean, you have money? Your money is *my* money."

"But you have so much of it, you can share with

your only daughter, can't you? I *am* your only child, aren't I?" It was childish, but at one point in time, I had thought he had another family because he was never around.

Now I knew why he was never around.

He sighed and ran his hands over his face. "You'll stay there or I will have to cut you off."

I gaped at him. Lucifer was loaded. He had multiple aliases throughout the world and the sum of his wealth was astronomical. It would put Bezos to shame.

"I'm not like them. They hate me because you're my dad and I don't even have wings to at least somewhat fit in." My voice caught in my throat and I fought to hold back tears. Lucifer didn't do well with tears. At least not from me.

"Danica... you don't need wings to fly."

"Don't go getting all mushy and philosophical on me." I laughed and wiped a stray tear that had fallen.

"I don't want this life for you." He gestured around him, referring to a life in hell. "At least try until the end of the semester. Maybe they just need time to adjust."

As much as I hated the idea of staying more time in this hell, I agreed. Maybe I just needed a way to relieve the stress this place was bringing me.

∾

AFTER I HAD cereal for dinner, because I most definitely wasn't going to eat in the dining hall, I drove about thirty minutes from the academy to a mall in Pasadena. I pulled my car into the parking structure and felt relief flood me. Shopping always cheered me up and I'd get to be around people who had no idea who I was.

As I made my way inside the mall, my phone buzzed with a text from Tobias. *Are you ok? I heard what happened.*

I shot a quick text back. *Fine. Shopping. I'll text you later.*

I'll admit it. I had a shopping problem. In particular when it came to a certain lingerie store. Their new line, with angel in the name of course, just released and I was beyond excited to add all the colors to my already vast collection.

The pink polka-dot walls and scents of fruit and floral instantly brought a smile to my face. I grabbed a mesh bag to put my bounty in and started with the panties.

"Can I help you find anything in particular?" I looked up and smiled at the saleswoman standing at the end of the display.

"No, thanks. I got it."

"Let me know if you need any help." She walked away but didn't go far before her eyes were watching me while she straightened panties and bras in the next display over. I guess I'd watch me too if I saw a teenager practically shoveling underwear into a bag.

Next time I'd just order online. There were eight colors. I had to have them all. As soon as I opened the drawers holding the bras the saleswoman approached me again.

I was starting to feel irritated. "You know what, you can help me." I handed her the bag. "Hold this for me."

I finished loading the bag up and made my way towards the cash register, but something caught my eye on a mannequin. Besides bras and panties, I'd never purchased anything else lingerie related. Teenage boys didn't really stop to appreciate what was under the clothes, but a certain man did.

It was a teddy that would have made a really inappropriate swimsuit with cutouts all over the front, lace to barely cover the important parts, and only strings in the back.

"Oh, that would look great on you," the saleswoman, who's name tag read Natasha, suggested. Now that she realized I wasn't going to make a run for it with the bag, she was my best friend.

"It's not something I normally wear." There was only red, white, and black so I grabbed the white. "I'd like to wear this one out of here."

Once I paid, the girl let me into one of the dressing rooms and I changed into it. Surprisingly, it was comfortable. I bit my lip thinking of what Tobias might think. Before I could talk myself out of it, I snapped a picture of myself, front and back, and sent Tobias the pictures.

After I put my clothes on over the teddy, I got a text back from him. *What time are you going to be back tonight?*

I sent back a devil and an angel emoji and put my phone away before I took things too far. The last thing I needed was to start sexting with him. Sending sexy pictures to my Demonology instructor was far enough already.

Leaving the store, I felt great. Nothing like a bag full of sexy things to give you a pick-me-up. I hopped on the descending escalator and looked out over the hustle and bustle of the evening mall. A baby cried in his mother's arms. A girl with a group of other teenagers shoved a corn dog in her mouth causing the other teens to laugh. A group of men leaned against the wall near a sports clothing store staring at their phones. I should have invited Brooklyn and Cora to shop with me.

There was something so normal about being here among the throngs of shoppers. Not having to worry what the Divine 7 might do next or what the other angels might say or do. If I left the academy, it could all be over. If I left then I wouldn't have money to shop. What a catch-22.

I hit a few more stores before encountering an arcade and getting sucked into the world of video games. If they could just find a way to teach school only using video games, I'd be set and have straight As.

"We're closing in like two minutes," a teenage boy about my age said, tapping on the side of Street Fighter II. I had been playing old-school games for hours.

I picked my bags up and made my way out into the mall, the stores already closed with rolling security grilles. The lights were dimmed and a few people milled about chatting, and some power walked like it was an indoor track. I looked at the time and it was just shy of eleven, the arcade had extended hours. I hadn't even realized I'd been playing that long. Amazing how video games seem to be on a different time continuum than real life.

I exited into the parking garage and took the elevator to the fifth floor. The doors slid open and I spotted my car, alone in the center of gray concrete walls and white lines. The echo of my shoes was the only sound besides distant screeching of tires on the floors below.

I was halfway to my car when the hairs on the back of my neck stood on end. I clutched my keys in my hand, my thumb poised over the alarm. I turned my head and looked over my shoulder. Nothing.

I wondered if men always felt like they had to look over their shoulders like women did. For once I would like to walk into a dark place and not wonder what lurked. The garage was eerily silent now, the only sounds the distant honking and whoosh of cars on the street below. I unlocked my car as I approached. And then I heard it.

It was the faintest sound, like leaves blowing across the pavement. My heart leapt into my throat as I threw open my car door and started lowering myself into the bucket seat with my bags drawn to my chest.

My head jerked back violently as a hand gripped my ponytail and pulled me back and up, my forehead hitting the edge of the car. My bags fell from my grip and onto the driver's seat and pavement next to the open door. A fine mist sprayed on my face, like water from a squirt bottle and I let out a scream as my head hit the pavement, sending a sharp pain through my skull.

There was no time to fight back. One second I was about to sit in my car, and the next I was thrown to the rough cement of the parking garage. My head went fuzzy and my eye sockets began throbbing. Another scream was lodged in my throat, but the only sound escaping me was short, rasping breaths.

Three men stood over me, their faces sneering and angry. They weren't that much older than me, but they looked rough, like they had lived twice or three times over. Two grabbed at my arms and legs. Adrenaline surged through me and I kicked and punched in a lame attempt at stopping them, but having just smashed my skull and there being three of them, I was up shit's creek without a paddle.

My crossbody purse lay under me, but nothing in there would help me. I didn't have pepper spray in my purse. It was in my car because the idea of it accidently exploding wigged me out. An irrational and stupid fear.

"Where the hell are her wings? Usually they pop out by now." The man not restraining me shoved a wadded-up cloth in my mouth before he zip tied my ankles and my hands.

"I don't fucking know, man. She hit her head pretty hard. Let's go."

The pressure of the zip ties dug into my skin and liquid dripped off of them, warming my skin where it touched. They picked me up like I was a trussed pig and carried me down the set of stairs near the elevator. A gray van waited with an open back door at the bottom of the stairs.

I'd never quite experienced true, all-encompassing fear before. Not the kind you have when you walk through one of the haunted houses at theme parks, or the kind you feel when the school resource officer's drug sniffing dog finds weed in your locker. No, this fear reached deep inside and made my teeth ache.

They threw me in the back of the van and slammed the door shut. I curled into a ball and coughed around the gag, my sobs making it hard to breathe. I tried spitting the rag out of my mouth but it just made me gag more.

I heard the front door of the van open and then a scream. Loud sounds and shouts erupted from outside and the van shook several times before everything was silent besides the small sounds escaping around my gag.

I had really reached my limit with the gags.

The door of the van opened and a fourth man looked down at me, shadows from the hood he was wearing hiding his face.

"I'm not going to hurt you." He had a blade and as he leaned in the bed of the van I kicked both legs out at him like I was a dolphin, connecting with his chest. He grunted but grabbed my legs anyway and cut off the zip tie. "Are you going to let me cut the one off your hands?"

I scrambled back away from him, trying to catch my breath through the gag and my running nose. I was going to die if I didn't get air. I might already be dead. My head felt like it was going to explode like a pumpkin smashed in the middle of the street.

The man waited while I looked at him with wide eyes. He had a bloody cut over his eye that was slowly trickling down his cheek and onto his black hooded sweatshirt. I could see the men who had attacked me laying in a heap just behind him. Literally, they were piled in a heap. Dead, I think.

Who was this guy? Batman?

I finally scooted forward because, between sobs and the gag, I was starting to feel dizzy, but that could have also been from hitting my head. I turned around and he sliced through the thick black plastic. I quickly yanked the cloth out of my mouth, taking in gulps of air.

He slid his knife behind him and raised his empty hands in front of him, backing up several feet from the van. I followed and sat on the edge, my hands on my knees, still trying to steady my heart and catch my breath.

"Who are you?" I managed to get out and stood up.

Standing up lasted all of three seconds before my knees gave out and my world went dark.

"LISTEN, *asshole*, I'm giving you the curtesy of a phone call so don't try to pull that bull shit with me... I told you, it was three Fallen... Yes, they were working together... Yes, I'm fucking sure... fuck you Toby, I'm not part of whatever it is they were up to, you should know that... Fine. I'll see you in five. Land on the roof, the door leads straight in."

My eyes opened and I let out a moan as the dim light in the room hit my eyes. My eyes quickly scanned what was in my line of sight. Brick walls, shiny duct work, giant industrial ceiling fan. My eyes were slightly blurred but beyond the black wire railing surrounding a bedroom of sorts, the room was massive. Then it became clear I was on a very large, very comfortable bed.

The vigilante snapped his eyes to the bed from where he was leaning against the railing and made his way to the side I was on. His bed. I was in Batman's bed.

"Your boyfriend will be here in a few minutes. I hope you don't mind. I got into your phone and since he was your last text, I called him." A smirk spread across his face as he spoke.

I should have known using a fingerprint to lock my phone was a stupid idea. It seemed safe at the time. He had called Tobias because of Tobias's text messages.

My eyes widened and the smallest of thrills shot through me knowing what the smirk was about. He had seen the last texts in my phone. I felt heat rising to my cheeks.

"I'm surprised you've been out so long. Usually angels heal up pretty quick." He placed my cell phone on the nightstand and ran his hands through his disheveled dark blond hair that came to his shoulders. "You want to try to sit up?"

I nodded, my brain not quite caught up yet with everything. I must have hit my head harder than I thought. He had saved me. Brought me to his home. Called... Toby?

I pushed myself up with a groan and scooted back against the pillows and metal headboard that matched the railing around the perimeter of the room.

"You know Tobias?"

I took a better look around. It was one giant open room with a kitchen, dining room, living room, and the bedroom. It appeared to be some kind of old building; the windows were similar to what an old warehouse or factory might have.

"Do I know Toby? You could say that. I'm Asher." He held out his hand and I put my hand in his.

His handshake was firm and sent tingles up my arm. Probably from the complete exhaustion my body felt. *Probably.*

"Danica." I let my hand fall to my lap and squinted my eyes up at him. He had a really sharp jaw and his eyes were a slate blue, almost gray. "You shouldn't have let me sleep so long. I think I have a pretty bad concussion. How long was I out?"

"About an hour. I honestly thought you'd be awake after a few minutes." He shrugged his shoulders and scratched the side of his scruffy face.

He stood awkwardly at the side of the bed like he wanted to sit but wasn't sure if he should. He finally sat at the end of it.

I stared at him for several long seconds before speaking. "They were fallen angels? The guys that attacked me? What did you do with them?"

"They were. I killed them so now they are dead. Probably in hell."

"I should call my dad so he can personally torture them." I flinched after the words left my lips. I wished sometimes I didn't just blurt out the first thing that popped into my head.

His eyes widened slightly, drawing my attention to where he had a small cut above his eye. He shifted a little and I could tell he was thinking about who my father was. Since I had such a damn big mouth, I told him.

"Lucifer is my father. I'm half human, half angel, or something. Do you think that's why the fallen attacked me?"

If my admission made him nervous he didn't let it show. "There was an attack a few days ago. Angels can sense each other. Fallen can't sense other angels very well but if they are close enough they can feel others."

"Is that why I feel all tingly and wired up when I'm around you or Tobias? No other angels have really gotten close enough to me."

Another one of his smirks spread across his face and he chuckled. "Tingly, huh? When I say *sense*, I mean our brains register another angel in the area and when we see them they have a glow about them."

If I could have died of embarrassment, I would have. I wasn't typically a blusher, but I felt my face burn red. Twice now he had made me blush.

Asher's chuckles abruptly stopped as the metal door across the room slammed open, causing him to jump. Tobias walked in and down the metal stairs. As soon as he got close enough, I could see the worry etched on his face.

He glared at Asher and then practically laid on top of me, pulling me into a hug.

"Are you okay?"

"Jesus, man. She isn't going to be if you manhandle her like that." Asher got off the bed and made his way down two steps and to the kitchen. He grabbed a glass that was half full of brown liquid and drank it in one gulp. Then he refilled it and did it again.

"My head hurts, but I'm fine. Thanks to Asher." I felt I needed to add that last bit because the tension was so thick you could have cut it with a knife.

"You're welcome," Asher said from across the room.

Tobias rolled his eyes at Asher's words and let me go before standing.

"Is her car here or back at the mall?"

"It's here. I drove her back in it. I also picked up all the lingerie that had spilled out of one of the bags and put them in the trunk," Asher said, making his way back to the bed and standing near the two steps leading down.

I wanted to crawl under a rock.

Tobias ignored Asher's comment and held out his hand. "Let's get you home."

I grabbed his hand and he pulled me to my feet.

He let go and my body plopped right back on the bed like my muscles and bones were made of jelly.

He tried to pick me up and I waved him away with my hand. My entire being ached and the thought of having to sit in a car and feel the movement and lights made me nauseous.

"She has a pretty bad concussion, and apparently she can't heal. Maybe she should stay here the rest of the night. I'll sleep on the couch. Or maybe *you* can sleep on the couch."

"Over my dead body." Tobias crossed his arms and turned his body towards Asher to glare at him.

Asher was purposely trying to piss off Tobias, but why? I hadn't known Tobias all that long but he was pretty calm, not letting his emotions explode. There was something about Asher though that was making him narrow his eyes and stiffen his spine.

"Have you forgotten already? Been there done that." Asher leaned against the brick wall behind him, propping one of his feet up with his knee bent like he had been waiting for this for a long time.

Tobias walked to the end of the bed and stopped at the end closest to Asher, clenching his fists at his sides. The last thing I needed was for them to come to blows and not even be able to break them apart. Not that I'd be stupid enough to throw myself in the middle of two men who probably knew how to throw punches.

"Guys, can you just put your dicks away for

now. You're making my headache worse. How do you two even know each other anyway?"

"You didn't tell her how you *died* yet? Shit, man. Seems like something you should tell the woman who's sending you sexy lingerie pics, doesn't it?"

Tobias moved so quickly it made my head hurt even more, and punched Asher in the jaw, sending his head to the side and back into the brick wall. He slid down the wall and sat on the floor rubbing his jaw, a smile on his face.

I shook my head and laid back down on the bed, kicking my shoes off. If they wanted to beat the shit out of each other, I really didn't care. All I wanted was to sleep.

Chapter Seven

Asher

*D*eath. It's something most angels have to go through to get to the angel part. Well, except for those created as angels. I didn't know what hell was like but being a fallen angel was not my cup of tea. In fact, most nights it was half a bottle of whiskey or a twelve pack.

It's hard for angels at first. Realizing our lives were ripped away from us, floating around in heaven, waiting for enough time to pass so we could make a choice. A choice to serve as a guardian on Earth or a choice to serve in heaven. I chose the former, by the way.

Any painful memories surrounding or leading up to our deaths are erased and all we're left with is the knowledge of how it happened and the memories of our life before. That's hard enough, the lost life.

Unless you're Fallen.

Then the missing memories come back.

Which is why I drink like a fish and fuck like a rabbit.

I looked over at Toby, who after sucker punching me in the fucking jaw, poured himself a whiskey without asking, and joined me on the large sectional sofa. I hadn't seen him in ten or so years and the first thing he does is punch me and steal my alcohol.

I really couldn't blame him for punching me though. I would have done worse, but I'm a dick. Tobias Armstrong is not. He is a saint, well, except for the student he seems to be sleeping with.

We fought together in World War II. He was like an older brother to me, taking me under his hypothetical, but now literal, wing. We survived D-Day, liberated towns, and died during the Battle of the Bulge.

It was cold that day, snow blanketing the ground when the Germans closed in on us. I don't even remember the exact date, not sure I even knew then what day of the week it was. Hell, it might have even been Christmas. We were well into the Battle of the Bulge though, and losing. At least we won the war. Well, the other soldiers did.

I stared down into my whiskey glass, Toby's presence bringing me back to that particular day.

. . .

"WE'RE GOING TO DIE, Toby. I don't want to fucking die." I was sniveling like a pansy-ass as debris, gunfire, and explosions rained down on our platoon.

"Shut up. We'll be fine. We've lasted this long." Tobias climbed back up the side of the bank and fired his gun. The sound was deafening. *"Fuck."*

I took his place as he reloaded his gun. This had been going on for what felt like hours, but was probably more like ten minutes. He'd shoot. I'd reload. I'd shoot. He'd reload. On and on it went. They kept advancing. My hands were numb, my shoulder throbbed, but on we went.

We had to. You don't watch most of your platoon die and just give up. We'd fight for them, for what they had lost.

I was out of ammo again and Toby went right back to his spot. I was just about done reloading when my body was thrown across the shallow agricultural trench we were using as a foxhole of sorts. It wasn't doing that good of a job, clearly.

My ears rang, my eyes burned, a blinding flash of pain careened down my back.

I'd told him we were going to die today. He didn't believe me.

A heavy weight landed on me and jerked several times before falling still.

I pried my eyes open and Toby stared back at me with wide, glassy eyes. Vacant eyes. Eyes I was too familiar with seeing. Another one of my brothers taken. I pushed at him, his body heavy.

"Toby?" I felt his hot blood seeping through my jacket and shirt. So much blood. Too much blood.

I needed to move. If the Germans decided to search the carnage, they'd take me. I didn't have it in me to be a prisoner. I struggled under Toby's weight, but I couldn't move my legs.

I stopped struggling and stared up at the gray sky. It would snow soon.

A HAND WAS PLACED on my shoulder and I jerked back to reality, sloshing the amber liquid in my glass onto my hand. Fucking idiot would know not to touch me if he had the memories of that shit storm. Lucky bastard.

PTSD was a mother fucking bitch and I couldn't even get help because who the fuck is going to believe that a mid-twenties looking man fought in WWII? Yeah. Exactly. No to the fucking one.

"Sorry, I shouldn't have-" He realized his errors a little too late.

"You're right, you shouldn't have." I leaned forward and set my glass on the coffee table before wiping my shaking, wet hand on my jeans. "So, you and Lucifer's daughter... interesting."

He made a grunting noise in reply and took a drink from his glass. He was still sitting next to me, he must have moved when I zoned out, a mere inch from my leg. I could have strangled his ass. I shifted farther from him.

I looked over my shoulder at her sleeping on my bed, her body curled around one of my pillows.

What would it be like to lay next to her and have her curl around me like that? Probably a really fucking bad idea is what it would be.

I looked over at my former best friend, my brother in arms. He was still rocking his beard, close shaven and neat. I hadn't known him before the war, but from the pictures he had shown me from before our time deployed together, he hadn't changed at all.

I, on the other hand, probably looked like a drunken vagrant. I used to be a handsome, strapping young fellow with hair like Cary Grant. The ladies loved me. Come to think of it, the ladies still loved me, and I still loved them. They just couldn't handle that I was completely fucking broken.

"You aren't worried they're going to take your wings? Banging a student has to be against some kind of rule."

"She's eighteen. We're both consenting adults. It doesn't matter if I'm a teacher or not." His words didn't hold any conviction and fell flat. He must have lay up at night convincing himself of those things.

I snorted back a laugh. "Keep telling yourself that. Trust me, you do *not* want to fall."

The worst part of falling wasn't losing use of the wings or any special abilities, it was the sudden bombardment of the memories and complete and utter isolation. Most didn't survive beyond the first few weeks, but those of us that did, were broken.

That's probably why the Fallen were trying to kidnap angels. I didn't even want to think about *why* they were kidnapping angels or what they were doing to them. I had stopped two abductions now and they had probably gotten away with several.

"I think it'd take a lot more than a relationship with a student to lose my wings. Don't you?"

"Just don't murder anyone you aren't supposed to and you'll be fine."

Killing as an angel was strictly forbidden. When we were given an assignment to help a human, it didn't mean taking the law into our own hands. Which is exactly what I did. I was supposed to help a woman flee, not kill her husband, even if he had beaten her black and blue.

"You've tried appealing?" Toby finally looked at me. He had been avoiding looking at me, probably because he felt pity. He sure as hell didn't feel guilty.

When I first fell, he came to see me to check on me. That didn't go so well. Hence why we hadn't seen each other in ten years.

"I gave up after the second appeal." I shrugged. "It is what it is. I'm getting things on track."

A comfortable silence fell over the room. The only sounds were the sips he was taking of his drink. I considered turning on the TV because I certainly wasn't going to be able to sleep now, but then he had to go and open his big-ass mouth again.

I had known the moment would come eventually. Ten years ago when I fell, he hadn't dared ask, especially as I tore up a motel room in a blinding rage.

"What happened?"

He didn't even have to elaborate. I knew exactly what he was asking. I stood and walked over to the kitchen, grabbing the bottle of whiskey that sat half empty on the counter. I sat back down in the crook of the sectional sofa, facing him, leg bent in front of me to give me a barrier. I'd kick his ass if he tried to touch me again. He reached over with his glass and I filled it back up.

"Do you want to know how you died or how I died?" I lifted the bottle to my lips and took a long swig. It burned more than usual tonight.

"Me."

I described the day to him, not leaving out any detail. The day was always vivid in my mind, even after all this time. Down to what we had eaten. What wasn't vivid was what I had eaten for breakfast that current morning. It's funny what the brain holds onto.

"Your body landed on mine. You died pretty instantly, lots of blood. I'm not sure if you landed on me because something threw your body at me or if you dived on top of me. Only you'd know that answer."

He ran his hand through his hair and we both took a drink at the same time.

"And you?"

I let out a pained laugh. "I wasn't as lucky as you were. I couldn't move from the waist down, so I was stuck there under you. It didn't exactly hurt. I was in shock that it was even happening. The pain only started when the snow started falling."

"Fuck."

"Yeah." I took another swig of whiskey and then put the cap back on. "I blamed you for a while."

"For what?" He seemed confused.

"For landing on me. I don't know what I would have done if I had gotten out from under you though. Probably would have been tortured by Krauts."

"It makes no sense." He wiped at his eyes as if he was about to shed some tears. He always was a sensitive bastard.

"What doesn't? It was war."

"I meant that it makes no sense to me that when an angel falls, something so traumatic and painful is given back to them."

"Maybe they figure it's better than sending us straight to hell. I can tell you it's probably not." As I spoke, I looked back over at Danica. I was still trying to wrap my head around that one.

"She's not... evil," he said softly.

"I didn't think she was. Lucifer is Fallen, right? He didn't have his death to torment him. That's probably why they stuck him for an eternity in hell. She didn't grow up in hell, did she?"

"Not literal hell. Her mom died when she was born and her dad could only be around so much. She got kicked out of high school."

I looked back over at her, feeling drawn to her. To make sure she was safe. I felt the tight muscles in my jaw relax and I let out a sigh.

"You feel it too, don't you?" Toby looked at me with a slight narrowing of his eyes, more of a thoughtful narrowing, as if he was running through things in his head. Not a narrowing like he was going to punch me again.

I knew exactly what he was talking about. It was what she had described when she told me what she thought sensing other angels was like. Tingly and almost giddy, and I never felt giddy.

"Yes. What is it?"

I didn't know whether to be concerned with it or accept it as normal. I should probably have been concerned. Even when I was an angel I had felt detached from everyone, missing my old life. My wife. My family. But around her I felt connected. They needed to seriously invest in training angel therapists.

"I'm not sure. There's someone else too, but she doesn't seem to be aware of it yet." He sounded jealous, but also angry. Before I could ask him why, he continued. "He bullies her. Him and his cronies."

"Why haven't you kicked his ass? If I could come to campus, I'd do it. Not like I have anything left to lose."

He rolled his eyes at me and I felt a warmness spread in my chest. This was familiar. Normal. How we used to be.

"He's an archangel. They sent him to us hoping we could acclimate him to how the world works. Plus, he was causing problems. I guess creating an archangel at the height of human times backfired a bit. I see the way he looks at her, yet he does stupid shit to her with his friends. Honestly, I don't even know if he realizes what he's doing, he just follows the other Divine like a lost puppy. And she just takes it and gives it back to them. She's strong, Asher. Stronger than I think she even knows." A dreamy look crossed his eyes but then he seemed to snap out of it and yawned.

"Why don't you go to bed." I grabbed my headphones off the table and turned them on, the Bluetooth connecting to my phone. Music helped me sleep. It was the only way I could sleep, actually.

"You going to be all right?"

"I'm not sure my jaw will ever be the same again, but I'll be fine, brother. Go lay next to your woman."

IT TOOK me a long time to fall asleep and at best I got three hours. Worse than usual, but at least not as bad as not being able to sleep for three days straight. That had fucking sucked.

The large metal barn door leading to the bathroom slid open and Danica walked out, looking much better than she had the night before. I had given her a shirt and a pair of sweats with an elastic and drawstring waist to wear after she showered. Her damp hair was gathered around one of her shoulders, making the dark fabric of the shirt even darker.

She looked stunning. Partly because she had my clothes on and there was something sexy about seeing a woman wearing my clothes. I turned away to not appear like I was gawking and filled my coffee maker up. I was probably going to drink a whole pot of it just to counteract all the whiskey I drank the night before.

"Where's Tobias?" Her voice was stronger today, less scratchy.

"He went to grab food. How do you like your coffee?" I grabbed a second mug from the open metal shelf and went to grab the carafe but stopped when I saw the scrunched-up face she was sporting.

"Poured down the drain. You don't by a slim chance have any Diet Dr. Pepper?"

Now I scrunched up my face. Gross. "You fucking drink that shit? And here I thought we were soul mates. I have orange juice, water, and liquor. Unfortunately, I'm out of beer."

"You sure do have a dirty mouth."

I raised my eyebrows. This was really the first real conversation I was having with her. Last night she was solely focused on her almost-abduction by three now-dead Fallen. I wasn't sure if her words meant she was appalled by my sailor's tongue or if she was poking fun at me.

I decided to test the boundaries a little. "Maybe I should show you just how dirty it can be." I licked my bottom lip for effect.

Her face turned pink and then she sat down on a stool around my stainless-steel bar-height table. "This is a cool place. Where are we, in an old warehouse?"

I took a drink of my black coffee and leaned against the counter. "It's an abandoned factory. There are two units downstairs I restored too that have tenants. I have an industrial chic remodeling business."

I looked around at the large open room. It had taken me several years to finish all the work myself, but it was a good distraction and got out some of my rage. Using my hands to tear down and then restore something helped keep my broken pieces from falling all over the place.

"Construction by day, vigilante by night?"

"Something like that."

The recent influx of Fallen encounters were concerning to say the least. We were a reclusive bunch, not often building long-term relationships, and most certainly not seeking companionship with each other. So the fact that I had encountered two groups of Fallen had me on edge.

Why were they after angels? Why were they using demon blood? Where were they getting the demon blood?

She cleared her throat and I blinked and looked at her. I spaced out a lot if I wasn't doing something with my hands. Luckily that time I was thinking about last night.

"You got into my phone last night." It was a statement. Did she want a response back? Luckily, she continued. "And you went through my photos."

I wish women would just spit out what their words meant. She was clearly unhappy with my intrusion, but just how unhappy? Slap me in the face unhappy? Kick me in the balls unhappy? Did she want an apology?

"I didn't go through your photos. I opened your texts to call whoever was sending you so many. He sent a lot. Did you read them yet? What a stalker. Better watch out for that one." I grinned around the rim of my coffee cup as her face looked a bit murderous. I guess she had wanted an apology. "Look, I'm sorry. I saw it was Tobias Armstrong and I scrolled up only meaning to see the ones he had sent. I was a little bit disappointed they weren't nudes, but they were hot nonetheless."

I was glad the table was between us. "You're an ass. You know that?"

"I am aware of that fact. So you and Toby?"

"Yeah. Me and Toby." She watched me as I refilled my cup. "So, how do you two know each other? I didn't get an answer before you got punched in the face, and since he left you here alone with me, I'm guessing you know each other well."

I laughed and sat at the table on the metal stool across from her. "World War II, same platoon. That's where we both died."

Her eyes went wide and then her expression softened. "I can't even imagine what it's like being in a war zone... and during a World War? Wow."

I expected her to ask more questions, but she didn't. I respected that. Maybe one day I'd tell her about my past life. I stood abruptly and my stool fell over, hitting the concrete floor with a loud metallic sound that made us both jump, and in my haste to flee, I fell flat on my ass over the stool.

Danica rushed around the table and I held up both hands in front of me. "Just give me a minute, okay?"

Where the hell had that come from? Telling someone about my life made my skin crawl. The last time I'd shared my life with someone, they had died, right the fuck on top of me. I shut my eyes and tried to remind myself that I was fine. I was safe here in my home. The home I'd built with my bare hands.

With slightly shaky legs, I stood and righted the stool before meeting her eyes. "I'm sorry about that. Sometimes it just comes out of nowhere."

Usually I could keep myself in check. So much

so that I was able to start my own business a few years ago. My workers all knew I suffered from severe PTSD, although they thought it was from Iraq, and on the days I couldn't handle things, they had my back.

Toby chose that moment to walk into my place, a pink box in one hand and a Diet Dr. Pepper in the other. His eyes went to Danica's worried face and then they shot quickly to me, concern etched in them.

"Everything okay?" He put the box and soda on the table slowly. "I got donuts."

It was like one minute there was tension in the air and the next her face lit up like a Christmas tree. She threw her arms around Toby like he had just come back from a long deployment and then they were kissing.

Oh, shit, were they kissing. If I opened the dictionary and looked up the term face-sucking, there would be a picture of them. I'd buy her every damn Diet Dr. Pepper and donut on the face of this planet if she'd kiss me like that.

Before I started thinking of her body pressed against me, her lips opening and waiting for my tongue, I lifted the lid of the donut box and the sweet sugary scent of maple and chocolate hit me right in the face. I grabbed the glazed twist with a hint of cinnamon woven into it and took a bite. A moan escaped my lips. I hadn't had a donut in a while.

Toby ripped his lips away from Danica's and looked at me with a glare as if I was inconveniencing his make-out session right in front of my fucking face.

I swallowed my bite and grinned at Toby's narrowed eyes. Serves him right for making out in front of me. "Want a bite?"

Toby rolled his eyes and then grabbed his own donut before sitting down. "What are we going to do about those Fallen?"

"Well, they are dead now and were disposed of. I didn't see who came and got them. I've searched the vans. There is nothing in them."

"Do you think there are more?"

I shrugged in response. "I guess we'll find out, won't we?"

"They sensed I was an angel. Said something about my wings not coming out when they sprayed me in the face." Danica nursed her Diet Dr. Pepper in her hands. I briefly wondered how addicted she was to it, having asked for it so early in the morning. I wasn't one to talk though. I had a bad habit of my own.

"Wait, why didn't your wings come out?" I looked back and forth between Toby and her.

"I don't have wings." I could tell immediately that it bothered her by the way her mouth turned slightly down and her eyes glossed up.

"Well, mine are bound so they can't come out. I guess we have something in common."

"That's horrible! All fallen angels have bound wings?" She looked back and forth between me and Toby. How did she know nothing about being an angel?

"Yes. It doesn't hurt. Well, until they really want to come out, then it feels like a dull ache in the shoulder blades."

"We should get going after we eat. I need to talk to Sue Whittaker about these attacks so she can get a message to Michael."

I grunted in response, my mouth full of donut. As much as I didn't want to admit it, the company was nice. Especially the brunette across from me, wearing my clothes. Lucky for me, I already programmed her number in my phone.

Chapter Eight

Danica

$\mathcal{I}$ stood frozen in front of the brightly colored paper taped to the hallway walls. There were so many, like rainbows leading down every hallway. The pot of gold at the end of the rainbow? My utter humiliation.

They had photocopied them all, all 'Notice of Disciplinary Action' forms and suspension forms, and plastered them around Uriel Hall. They were all there.

Caused physical injury to another person.

Unlawful use of an illegal substance.

Disruption of school activities.

There were so many in my file over the years that I didn't even remember most of them. I clutched my bag to my chest and made my way out of the building, keeping my eyes on the ground.

How dare they.

How dare they take something that was in my past and put it out there for the world to see? Wasn't it enough that I was here, at this school, *trying?*

I threw my bag on the floor and faceplanted onto my bed. I shut my eyes, breathed in deep, and exhaled. I could do this. I'd go back in there and take them all down once classes were in session.

My phone buzzed in my bag and I groaned. *Tobias.*

He had taken care of me all weekend. We never went on our date. Instead, he cooked for me in his room. Chicken fettuccini alfredo. Salad. Garlic bread. I felt my chest tightening and I swallowed back my tears. At some point he was going to realize that I came with a lot of baggage.

I rolled off my bed and grabbed my phone. *Don't come to class.* As if that warning would stop me in the first place.

Me: Too late for that. Still want to date a juvenile delinquent?

Tobias: Don't say that.

I turned off my phone and changed out of my uniform. It was a little chilly outside so I threw on sweats and a hoodie. I wasn't technically going to class, so no uniform was required.

It took me most of the morning to take down all of the papers spread around campus. Mainly because I hid between class times. I'd save my brave face for tomorrow. Adults are always saying to just ignore the bullies, but did that actually work? This was something deeper. This was a deep-seated hatred for Lucifer and for me. What had the devil ever done to them?

I wanted to punch each and every one of them in their glowing faces. Or leave. Leaving would be better, but part of me didn't want to leave. One thing was clear, something needed to change or I wasn't going to make it to the end of the semester.

I HID in my room the rest of the day until my last class; independent study in the library. Except now Mondays would be dedicated to peer mentoring. What that entailed hadn't exactly been made clear to me. Or maybe it was, and I had zoned out as Dean Whittaker had droned on and on.

At least my day was going better, especially after the picture Tobias sent me. Normally a dick pic would turn me off, but if anything, it just made me want him more. I'd always laughed at the movies or books where the girl falls head over heels after a few days. I understood now. When it was there, it was just *there*.

Although, a certain dirty-mouthed vigilante kept popping into my head as well, but that was probably something for a therapist to explore.

I plopped down in a leather armchair in the corner of the library and tipped my head back to let the light from the colonial-style window hit my face. What I would give to be napping right now. With a long exhale, I sat up and dug in the front section of my bag for the tiny pouch with my Flair pens. They were my version of a fidget spinner; constantly switching pens helped my focus. Plus, they made my notes look like a rainbow threw up on them. A win in my book.

They were nowhere to be found though. Hopefully they were back in my room. Or had I left them in a class? Shrugging to myself, I dropped my bag on the floor and scanned the library. It was empty as usual. Ms. Hall was just out of my line of sight, her long manicured nails creating a very faint tapping sound on her keyboard. Hopefully this week wouldn't be a repeat of last week.

The heavy wooden library door opened and I turned my head towards it.

No. Just no.

I pressed my lips together and gripped the arms of the chair, digging my fingernails into the leather. If I hadn't known him already, I would have sat up straighter, pushed my chest out, smoothed down my clothes. Then worried about my choice in wearing sweats.

Oliver Morgan was breathtaking.

He walked towards me, his lips quirked into a small smile, his blue eyes appraising my sweats. He sat down in the chair next to me and turned to face me, touching the top of his brown hair as if to check that the hair product that held it in place was still working.

I pursed my lips and crossed my legs. "Well, isn't this fucking fantastic."

He shrugged his shoulders and tilted his chin in the direction of my bag while he shrugged out of his blue blazer and laid it over the arm of the chair. The faint smell of chocolate chip cookies hit my nose.

"Did you bring the binder?"

"What binder?" My eyebrows drew together and I tilted my head slightly to the side. "Was I supposed to bring stuff?"

"The school handbook binder. Dean Whittaker said she told you to bring it with you. That's what we're going to be going over." He crossed his arms behind his head and leaned back against the back of the chair.

"Oh... I forgot."

He shut his eyes and opened them in an extra-long blink and then leaned forward again to pull his binder out of his bag. "Let's just get this over with."

He moved his chair so our knees were practically touching and opened the binder, placing it on my lap. He pointed to the first line in the table of contents. Dress code.

"Is this really necessary? I can just read it on my own." I leaned my elbow on the side of the chair and put my cheek on my fist.

He grunted and flipped the pages open to the

dress code section. He then reached into his bag and pulled out a notebook and a pen and handed them to me. I ran my hand over the smooth cover of the notebook that had a pink watercolor design and a gold embossed D on it. The pen was thicker than usual, given it had ten retractable colors.

"What's this for?" I shifted in my seat. I was kicking myself for the flutters in my stomach. Why had he given me something so... personalized?

He let out a breath and pinched the bridge of his nose. "Notes. Remember you'll have a test at the end of our mentoring sessions."

"Right... So, dress code." I flipped open the small notebook and labeled the first page. "Rule 1. Wear ridiculous sailor uniforms because we're children that can't dress ourselves. Is that correct?"

"Are you going to take this seriously? We wear uniforms so we aren't distracted from our studies. God only knows what you would wear if you were given free rein." He looked at my sweats with a raised eyebrow.

I pushed down hard with my pen as I wrote. He leaned forward again and looked at the page, nodding his head slightly. I didn't know how he could read upside down; I sure couldn't. I clicked the pen a few times and drew several swirly circles on the corner of my paper.

"Are you listening?"

My head snapped up and I pulled the notebook

towards my chest. "I umm... no. I wasn't listening. I mean, I was but..."

He tapped a finger on his lips before sitting back in his chair, his legs moving out from where they were against the bottom of the chair and touching mine.

"Is your endgame to go to hell and work with your father? Really, you punched a guy because he gave you a church paper or something?" His eyebrows furrowed and he reached forward and grabbed the pen I continued to click.

I looked down at the binder on my lap and brushed away an imaginary piece of eraser shaving. He didn't say anything during my silence, the only noise in the room the faint sound of steps in the hall and the printer at Ms. Hall's desk spitting out papers.

He broke the silence by nudging my foot with his, causing my head to snap up. He looked back at me, his light smattering of freckles even more prominent in the slant of light from the window.

"That is what happened, right?" He put the pen back in the middle of the binder.

"He did give me a church flier, so that's what the principal chose to believe."

He cleared his throat and sat up straighter. I could tell he really wanted to ask more questions. Only Ava and I knew the truth, and we wanted to keep it that way. We had heard rumors that those who knew and didn't join were beaten to a pulp.

I closed the binder and handed it back to him while grabbing my bag off the floor. I quickly stood while unzipping it and dropping the pen and notebook inside.

"Where are you going? We have fifteen more minutes. If Dean Whittaker-"

"I don't give a shit about Dean Whittaker or any of this. You sitting here acting like you care is a joke." My eyes darted to the door and then back to him.

He looked up at me with downturned lips and stood. "At least stay in the library so if she comes by you don't get in more trouble."

"Fine," I said through gritted teeth before turning and making my way down the rows of books labeled *Angel History*.

I grabbed a random book off a shelf and started flipping through it, stopping to look at the pictures. What was I even looking at? I slammed the book shut and read the title on the cover: *Angel Disgrace During the 1970s*. I snorted back a laugh.

"It is funny, isn't it? That they'd put that crap in a book for everyone to see."

I turned and rolled my eyes as Oliver leaned on the sturdy wooden shelf next to me. He plucked the book from my hands, frowning.

"I wonder what they'll write about me." He flipped through the book in the same way I had, furrowing his brows.

"Probably that you're an asshole that picks on the weak."

"You aren't weak. Your actually pretty strong." He shut the book with a snap and reached past me and put it on the shelf, his shirt sleeve brushing against my shoulder.

"Oh, so that's what all the bullying is for? To test my strength? You know what? I'm actually glad because now I get to see what phonies you all are. My dad is more angel than any of you."

I straightened my back and stared up at Oliver. I hadn't realized he was so tall, the top of my head coming to his chin. Someone knew what they were doing when they created him.

He stared back down at me and leaned closer.

"Maybe you're right," he said gently.

And then he kissed me.

I LAID on the soft comforter of my bed, the slight breeze outside wafting in and brushing across my skin. My lips still tingled from Oliver's very short, yet satisfying, kiss. One second his lips were on me and the next he was out the door. My mind was swirling as I brought my fingers to my lips.

The kiss had lasted only for a few seconds, but a few seconds I couldn't take back. It sent a thrill through me, kissing him there against the shelf in the library, each breath smelling of books and the faint scent of chocolate chip cookies.

Honestly, I felt a little like a harlot. Three men had occupied my mind today and I couldn't stop thinking about my body pressed up against them, their hands roaming my curves, their lips on my-

My phone buzzed on my chest and I lifted it above my face to read a text from Ava. My head hurt. Maybe my heart hurt a little too. Oliver Morgan had kissed me. And I kissed him back.

I had been texting Ava all evening about my confusion.

Aren't you sick of idiot boys? I vote for the teacher. He's a man.

She had a point, but would that even work? He was absolutely the most attentive guy I had ever been interested in. He had even left a can of soup, box of crackers, and bottle of 7 Up outside my door. I felt only slightly guilty that my stomachache had been a lie to be left alone.

I think he stole my panties.

So? That's hot. What do you think he did with those panties? He's probably not wearing them if that's what you're thinking. She followed her text with an eggplant emoji. Ava wasn't so innocent after all.

A laugh bubbled out of me. *Wow. No words.*

I need to tell you something... about John.

My stomach dropped and I sat up. I could see she was typing out a text so I waited. My hand shook slightly.

That day you punched him, Officer Flores took that flier off the ground. I'm not sure what happened exactly, but him and his dad were arrested over the weekend.

I let out a long, shaky breath of air. I knew exactly what happened. His father's drug mule business, hidden behind the veil of being a church, had imploded. Him giving me the flier like that was a threat to me to work for them or be sacrificed. When John gave you a flier, there was no choice.

I knew I should have never bought my weed from him in the first place, but I had needed it and it was high quality. If I had known they were more than just weed dealers, I would have found someone else.

My phone buzzed and another text popped up with an unknown number. I opened it and a smile spread across my face.

Asher: Hey, this is your knight in shining armor, Ash. How is your head?

Me: It's feeling better. If angels weren't such dicks it would be even better.

Asher: I won't disagree with that. What happened? Whose ass do I need to kick?

I laughed, a smile plastered on my face. *Everyone's.*

Asher: Even Toby's?

Me: What are you up to tomorrow? I'm thinking of ditching classes...

Asher: Work. I usually go to the pool hall or a bar after.

I bit my lip and went to stand by the window,

looking out over the darkened campus. There were several angels milling about and one on the far side, across the far field, going into the trees.

Me: Let's hang out. Ditch work.

Asher: Can't do that but maybe when I get home. Meet at my place at 5ish?

Me: Yeah, see you then.

Now I was going to get no sleep because I was sleeping with a teacher, kissing my bully who bought me a personalized notebook and pen, and hanging out with a Fallen.

Chapter Nine

I must have been overzealous about hanging out with Asher because I got to his place before he did. I sat at the top of the metal stairs that led to his door and tried to calm the fluttering in my stomach.

This was just two friends hanging out. Right? Not that he was a friend yet, he was Tobias's long-lost Fallen friend. Tobias was surprisingly understanding, or at least he appeared that way when he stopped by after classes to check on me. I couldn't keep this from him, especially given their history. Which was still a big fat mystery to me. There had to be more to their stories than just that they had fought and died together in WWII.

Nothing was ever so cut and dry.

"A woman that's on time, I like that."

My eyes snapped to the bottom of the stairs and

I stood, tugging my shirt so it fell back into place. I hadn't even heard him drive up in his truck.

"Or I just got lucky. There was no traffic." I adjusted the strap of my purse on my shoulder. God, why was I so nervous?

He smiled and slid his sunglasses on the top of his head. His hair was pulled back into a small man bun, which worked for him, and his face was cleanly shaven. I tried to hide the fact that my eyes ran down his body, taking in his opened blue plaid flannel, gray shirt, blue jeans, and work boots marked with dirt. The flirty smirk on his face told me I didn't do a good job.

"I hope you don't mind if I shower first." He brushed past me and opened his door, holding it open. "I'm assuming you don't want me to smell."

I smiled at him as I squeezed past him and took in the clean space. The other day it had clothes thrown over a chair and floor, and empty bottles and food containers covering the counters. It had looked like he hadn't cleaned in weeks.

"You didn't have to clean for me."

"Who said I cleaned for you?" He bumped my shoulder playfully as he passed and went to the kitchen. "Drink?"

I watched as he poured himself a glass of whiskey and then went to the refrigerator. "I've got wine, beer, Diet Dr. Pepper."

My heart fluttered. He had said Diet Dr. Pepper

was crap, but he had stocked his fridge with some. "I'll take some wine."

He turned and raised his eyebrows but then pulled a bottle of white wine out and grabbed a wine glass out of a top cupboard. He probably didn't use the wine glasses often.

He walked over to where I had perched on the arm of the couch and held the half-filled glass out to me. I reached out to take it, our fingers touching, but he didn't let go. His slate blue eyes, a little bluer than the other day, stared down at me, then at my lips. My legs spread slightly and he took a small step forward.

"I should go take a shower." His voice had taken on a slightly husky quality but then he stepped back and pulled his sunglasses off the top of his head. "Make yourself at home."

I let out a shaky breath after he slid the bathroom door shut and sat down on the couch. All I could think about was him in the shower. Did the muscles in his forearms extend under his shirt? Did he have any tattoos?

Never before had I longed for three guys. I hated admitting to myself that there were three but I couldn't stop thinking about chocolate chip cookies. Two were probably more man than I could handle, and then there was Oliver. I didn't even know how old he was. He was around my age, but he was a Class I angel, which meant he just *was*.

Tobias and I hadn't talked about *us*. The idea of

being a couple was too new. We barely knew each other. But he hadn't said anything about me wanting to hang out with Asher. Because that's all this was, two people getting to know each other as friends.

I sipped the wine, the faint hint of fruit staying on the back of my tongue. I didn't usually like wine, but this almost tasted like juice. I turned on the TV to some court show and only half paid attention until the bathroom door slid open.

The soft scent of coconut and pineapple wafted into the room. Asher did not strike me as the tropical scent type, but I wasn't complaining. I turned my head and watched as he walked out with a towel around his waist, his lean, toned body on full display. I raised my wine glass to my mouth and took a prolonged sip as he walked up the two steps to the bedroom platform to a chest of drawers, his back turned towards me. He had a large tattoo of black wings covering the entirety of his back and part of his arms.

Holy mother of all things holy.

I turned so my leg was bent on the couch and watched as he dropped his towel and pulled a pair of blue jeans from a drawer. I didn't know if he thought I wouldn't look or if he was purposely baring his toned ass.

My wine was gone, but my lips were still on the rim of the glass as he slid the jeans on with no underwear. Tobias wasn't too keen on wearing them either. The jeans hit just below the two dimples in his lower back.

Quickly turning back towards the TV so I wouldn't be caught, I put my hand on my chest to try to calm myself down. The judge on TV was lecturing a couple for wasting her time with nonsense.

I didn't look away from the TV until he walked into the kitchen, buttoning the last button on his green plaid shirt, but leaving the top two undone. He grabbed the whiskey he had left on the kitchen table and drank it all at once.

"Ready to go? I was thinking we could check out this new Korean barbecue place a few blocks from here."

He offered me his hand and I took it as I got up off the couch. His callused hand was massive compared to mine and made me feel... safe. I followed him as we made our way down the stairs, still letting him hold my hand.

DINNER WAS INTERESTING. Not interesting in a bad way, but in a 'holy shit is he flirting with me?' and 'please, keep your leg pressed against mine' kind of way. We talked about almost everything. Food, his business, my school issues past and present, interests.

He threaded his fingers through mine, looking

over at me as we made our way back down the street towards his place. The whole area was being revitalized by people like him, turning previously abandoned buildings into lively hot spots and living spaces.

"Are you going to come up or head back to school?" He had finally let my hand go and had his arm slung around my shoulder, his fingers playing with my hair. I was glad I had chosen at the last minute to wear it down.

I wasn't cold but had goosebumps on my skin from his touch. Did I want to go up to his place with the bed and the couch all in the same room, beckoning me? *Yes.* Should I? The jury was still out on that one.

I looked up at him, the white strand lights in the trees lining the street creating a soft glow on the sidewalk. His eyes sparkled and looked back at me, darkened with dilated pupils. What would it be like to have his strong, callused hands on my skin?

His hand tightened on my shoulder and he stopped, his neck stiffening and his eyes darting to the other side of the street.

"Stay right here." He moved me in front of a large window of a restaurant, the couple sitting on the other side glancing briefly at us before going back to their conversation. "I need to go check something out."

Before I could protest or ask any questions, he jogged across the street, stopping in the middle on the dashed yellow lines to wait for passing vehicles. I watched the space between two buildings he had disappeared between with a frown and then made my way across the street. It led to an alley that ran behind the buildings. I strained to hear but the only sounds were the passing of cars and the noises coming from the restaurants and bars lining the street.

On impulse, I quickly walked down the path between the buildings and peeked around the corner. My eyes widened as Asher threw a man in dark clothing into another and they fell onto the ground. He walked with clenched fists and hunched shoulders to the nearest one, grabbed his head and snapped his neck. The sound caused me to gasp and cover my mouth with my hand.

He grabbed the next man who was scrambling back like a crab and did the same thing. He piled the two limp bodies on top of a third near the wheel of the gray, windowless van blocking the alley.

I felt as if my heart was going to jump out of my chest cavity and explode. I stepped out of the darkened walkway as Asher pulled open the back doors of the van.

"I told you to stay across the street." He didn't look in my direction as he reached into the van and dragged two angels out; one had their wings extended and arms and legs zip tied, but the other didn't.

I took another step forward and gasped as they stepped into the light from a lamp post. I rushed forward and knelt by Oliver's side. He looked at me with wide eyes and tried to talk through his gag. I pulled it out.

"They came out of nowhere!" His voice was frantic and he smacked the ground with his wings, trying to sit up with his bound legs and arms.

I looked over at Asher who was staring down at Levi with a glowing silver weapon gripped in his hand. He looked confused and then turned towards Oliver and me.

"I take it you know these idiots?" Asher swiped the knife through Oliver's ties. "I'd never expect an archangel along with another angel to get taken by three Fallen. You should have felt them coming."

"We... we thought it was you two. They knocked us out before we even knew what hit us," Levi said, standing and reaching over to help Oliver up. I watched with rapt attention as Oliver shook out his shining wings and they folded back and disappeared.

Asher tucked his knife into the waist band of his pants near his hip, the faint sound of it sliding inside a sheath bringing my attention completely back to him.

"You're fucking idiots. What do they teach you at that school of yours? Fallen angels feel different." He shook his head and then turned towards me, putting his hand on his hips. "And I told you to stay back. Isn't one kidnapping attempt enough? What if they-"

"Who are you? You feel like those three... hey, where did they go?" Oliver moved his head around, looking for the heap of bodies that had suddenly vanished. He swatted Levi's chest with the back of his hand. "See. I told you following her was a bad idea."

Faster than my eyes could track, Asher had Oliver pinned against the side of the van, his feet dangling a foot off the ground. His jaw was set tight. "You were following her?" His words came out clipped and menacing.

Heat bloomed between my legs. Clearing my throat, I stepped forward and placed my hand on Asher's tense biceps.

"Let him go, Ash. It's okay." I didn't want Asher to kill them. I was curious as to why they had been following me though.

I turned to Levi and raised my eyebrows. Behind me I heard Oliver grunt as he dropped to the ground.

Levi sighed and ran a hand over his forehead. "He- we were worried. You missed class two days in a row."

My stomach clenched and I folded my arms over my chest. "You were *worried*. After all the bull-shit over the past week, are you really surprised?"

"These are two of the fuckers that have been assholes? Say the word and I'll kick their asses."

Asher took a step towards Levi who promptly backed up with his hands in front of him, palms out.

"We're sorry, we..." Oliver looked over to Levi and then at me. "We were stupid."

"That's an understatement." Asher grabbed my hand, lacing his fingers through mine.

Oliver's eyes looked down at our interlocking fingers and then up at me. His eyebrows arched and his frown deepened.

"You said that she was almost kidnapped?" Levi moved next to Oliver, keeping a wide distance between himself and Asher.

"Yes. There were three of them, same type of van. Why couldn't you guys get away?" I asked.

"Besides the demon blood on the zip ties, they spray something in your face. I think it makes you weaker. That's why I need my seraph blade to cut the ties," Asher explained while pulling his phone out of his back pocket. "I'm calling Tobias to come get you two. The demon blood that got on your skin will take a few hours to wear off. You won't be able to fly."

"Armstrong? Please don't!" Oliver took a step forward before Levi put an arm out across his chest, stopping him.

"Don't, Ash. I'll take them back." It was out of my mouth before I even knew what I was doing.

Asher turned to look at me and I crossed my arms under my breasts. He clenched his jaw. He put his phone back in his back pocket and muttered something unintelligible under his breath before turning and walking down the gap between the buildings we had come down.

We walked in uncomfortable silence back to his house, the two angels following us. When we reached my car, he looked past me across the street, his jaw set tight, moving slightly.

"I'll see you later." He leaned forward and brushed his lips against my cheek, the skin burning under the softness of his lips. He turned and headed towards the stairs leading up to his place.

I watched as he went and blinked several times, quelling the tears that had formed. He was disappointed our night hadn't ended well. I can't say I blamed him. I had wanted to go up those stairs with him.

We piled into my car, Levi in the back and Oliver in the front, and rode back to the school in silence.

～

WE SOMEHOW ALL ENDED UP IN Levi's room, which looked exactly like mine. So much for telling myself living in the staff building was a *good* thing. The only good thing about it was Tobias was right down the hall.

We sat in a circle on Levi's bed with a bottle of

vodka. How Levi had gotten a bottle of vodka was something I would file away to explore later.

"Let's play Never Have I Ever," I said after Levi had suggested playing Try Not to Laugh.

I'd have a hard time with that one and end up drunk before I even knew what happened.

"How do you play that?" Oliver was examining the text on the label of the vodka before he handed it back to Levi.

"You say something you've never done that you think the other players have done. If they've done it, they take a drink."

"Is it safe to drink a lot of that?" Oliver had a crease between his eyebrows and was frowning at the blue bottle.

I shrugged and looked to Levi who regarded Oliver with a smile and a twinkle in his eye.

"Olly here has never drank before. We always try to get him to but he won't." He handed the bottle back to Oliver. "You start."

"Okay, let's see. Never have I ever had alcohol?" He looked back and forth between us, seeking confirmation he was playing right.

"Good job, angel. You catch on quick." I snatched the bottle out of his hands and twisted the top. After taking a quick swig, I passed it to Levi, who I was certain had had alcohol before. Why else would he have three different bottles hidden under his bed?

"I'll go next," he said, wincing after taking a drink, "Never have I ever smoked weed."

I snorted and reached for the bottle but he tipped it back and took a drink before handing it to me. I narrowed my eyes slightly at him before grabbing the bottle and doing the same, my eyes staying locked on his hazel green ones.

"Never have I ever... been to heaven." Levi snatched the bottle back from me and drank before handing it to Oliver.

Oliver looked down the opening of the bottle and then took the smallest sip I had ever seen. I laughed at his puckered expression before he coughed and then took another small sip.

"God, it burns! How can you stand it?"

"You'll see once you get enough of it in you." Levi wiggled his eyebrows and touched my knee. "Right, Dee?"

"Right." I wasn't sure I liked him calling me Dee, it felt wrong. I tilted my head slightly to the side and looked at Levi. Really looked at him. He was kind of cute with his messy curly hair on top of his head and high cheekbones, but maybe the alcohol was already speaking to me.

"Never have I ever..." Oliver bit his lip and looked between us, seeming unsure of himself. "Had sex."

I threw my head back and laughed, not at him, but at myself, because boy, had I had sex. Would have probably done it with Asher had they not ruined our evening. I snatched the bottle and took a mouthful and looked at Levi. He took the bottle and drank.

"Really?" Oliver looked equally as surprised as I was.

"I was sixteen when I died. I had a girlfriend. Plus, Delilah and I hooked up once. Never have I ever lusted after more than one person at a time." He took another drink and then preemptively handed the bottle to me.

"You're playing wrong, Levi. You're supposed to say something you haven't done or felt." I took a drink and then Oliver reached over and grabbed it.

As he took a surprisingly long drink, his eyes danced between me and Levi. *Oh, fuck.* When I had taken a drink, I had thought of him, Asher, and Tobias. He was thinking of me and Levi.

He cleared his throat. "Never have I ever wanted to kiss someone in this room." He took another long drink and held it out to Levi with a shaking hand.

I would have never expected this game to take this turn with the angels who had been assholes to me, but here we were, already onto sex. Levi drank.

"Never-" he started, but I grabbed the bottle and took one shot while I looked at Oliver.

Yeah, I did want to kiss Oliver again, but I also wanted to smack him. He was a Grade A asshole, but damn if I didn't want him. What the hell was wrong with me?

"Never have I ever regretted being such an asshole more than right now." I smirked and handed the bottle to Oliver.

They both drank and Levi leaned over and put the bottle on his nightstand. "I think if we play anymore right now, Olly might puke."

I looked at Oliver with his glossy eyes and smiled. He was literally beaming. His faint glow was brighter than usual. He looked at my lips and I ran my tongue along them, causing him to suck in a breath of air.

I leaned forward and our lips connected, both of us letting out moans as the connection we had felt in the library took over our bodies. Maybe it was because he was an angel, but if all angels got this response from my body, I was in big trouble.

My hands moved to his shoulders and I pushed him back, lying on top of the hard contours of his body. His arms went to my hips, gripping lightly at first before the deepening of our kiss moved them to my ass.

He rolled us so he was on top and moved his lips to my neck where he delivered kisses so light across my throat that it felt like he was running feathers across my skin. I moaned and opened my eyes to see what had happened to Levi. He had laid next to us, his head propped up on his hand. His eyes locked on Oliver. My attention went back to Oliver as he recaptured my lips and parted them with his tongue. His tongue collided with mine and

I moved my hips up, connecting with his erection. He moaned against my lips.

"Take her shirt off." Levi's voice broke our kiss and we both looked at him.

I had just enough alcohol in me to throw caution to the wind. I was game if they were. Oliver was still staring at Levi as I reached down and tugged my shirt up as far as I could before he moved so I could remove it. Oliver looked down at my lace-covered breasts and let out a breath of air.

"Kiss them." Levi ran his free hand through his hair before lowering it to his pants and rubbing his evident erection through the fabric of his jeans. "Don't just stare at them."

Oliver took his finger and traced it over the top of my breasts before lowering his lips to kiss where he had just touched. I tilted my head back and then turned my head towards Levi and bit my lip. I wasn't attracted to Levi in the same way I was to Oliver, but part of me was curious what would happen.

He scooted forward and ran a finger along my bottom lip and then kissed me with such heat that I clenched my legs together, trying to lessen the over-whelming need that consumed me.

How would I even handle two guys at a time? One was hard enough as it was.

Levi moved his hands behind me, Oliver preoc-cupied with the swell of my breasts over the fabric of my bra. The restrictiveness of the bra went away as Olly kissed down my arm as he moved the strap down. I threw the bra to the side and watched as both guys looked at me with hunger in their eyes.

Oliver moved first, taking my left nipple in his mouth and sucking lightly. I arched my back and tangled one of my hands in his hair. Levi kissed my neck and trailed his tongue down to the same breast. He hesitated for a brief moment before he moved his lips near Oliver's.

Their lips met on my nipple and they both sighed against my skin. My hands threaded in Levi's soft curls as his lips and Oliver's began kissing around my nipple. It was hard not to watch and even harder to ignore how turned on I was by it. One of Levi's hands snaked around Oliver's neck and pulled him up towards him, their lips colliding in a needy kiss above me that had me feeling a little jealous.

Oliver broke the kiss and stared panting at Levi before his eyes cut to mine.

"It's okay." I looked between the boys and saw the lust in Levi's eyes, but not for me, for Oliver.

"I should go." Oliver slid off the bed and had his feet shoved in his shoes before we could react. "I'll see you guys in class tomorrow."

The door shut with a click and Levi rolled over and threw his hands over his face. Now that Oliver had left the room, my need to be touched evaporated.

Chapter Ten

I put my pillow over my face and pressed it against my ears. After Oliver's exodus the night before, Levi and I drank until we were sloppy drunk. Not my finest moment. The realization that Levi didn't turn me on was like a slap to the face. It was like all desire had evaporated once Oliver left. For a moment I had thought all angels that had dicks were going to turn me on.

I somehow managed to make it back to my room, but now someone was knocking on my door. I threw my pillow and pushed myself up. I was never going to drink again. How many times had I said that before?

My feet dragged across the floor, my eyes not quite all the way open, and I peeked out the peep-hole. I let out a groan because I really didn't want to see *him* right now. I turned the lock anyway and shuffled back to my bed, lying face down to block out the light that was making my eyeballs throb like someone was pumping them full of air.

The door opened with a small creak and clicked shut. The bed dipped as Tobias laid down next to me and pulled me towards him, the faint scent of mint hitting my nose.

"Time to wake up," he said, kissing my hair. I grumbled into his chest and shook my head. "Where were you last night? I called, texted, knocked. Asher called and told me what happened."

His hand went to my lower back and ran back and forth across it, sending tingles up my spine. Where the heck was my shirt? I didn't even remember taking it off. Besides making out and the hot kiss between Levi and Oliver, I didn't remember much else.

"I think I'm still drunk." I hiccupped and let out another groan as the jolt of the hiccup sent a pain through my skull. "Didn't mean to worry you."

"You got drunk with Oliver and Levi?" I nodded my response into his button up shirt and ran my hands over the smooth material on his back.

He pulled back so he could see my face. I bit my lip and saw the question in his eyes.

"We kissed. A lot." I flinched with my words. It was one thing to hold hands with Asher and flirt all night, but to make out with not one, but two different guys? Guilt was a fickle beast and it had currently set up shop in my chest. What Tobias and

I had was so new, yet I felt as if I had just cheated on a long-term love.

His hand moved a stray piece of hair out of my eyes and then rested on my cheek. "They've bullied you."

"I know." I looked at the top buttons on his shirt. "But I feel something for Oliver. I don't know what it is. Safety? I feel the same thing with you. With Asher. I know it sounds crazy."

He put his finger under my chin and tilted it up to meet my eyes. "It doesn't sound crazy. I feel the same way, and I bet if you asked them they'd say the same. What about Levi?"

I shrugged. "I probably wouldn't make out with him sober." I played with a loose thread on one of his buttons, tempted to yank on it, but not wanting to pop the button off. "I can't be with all three of you, that's..." He put his finger over my lips, stopping my words.

His eyes closed and he spoke softly. "I've been around a long time, both as a human and angel, and I have never felt like this. I'm not willing to let you go because you feel the same thing with them."

I kissed his finger and turned my head so it was on my cheek. "What about divinity points?"

He chuckled and opened his eyes, amusement written on their glistening surface. "Your dad really didn't explain anything to you did he? You being with us hurts no one. The only person you'd be hurting is yourself. Besides, divinity points really just help you get better guardian gigs." He kissed my cheek and then sat up. "Now, let's get you showered and to class because you *will* be going to class today even if I have to drag you there myself or throw you over my shoulder."

"Is that an offer to help me shower?" I rolled onto my back and looked up at him standing over me. His eyes moved down to my chest and narrowed slightly. My eyes fell to my left breast and I let out a groan. "Yeah, about this." I ran my finger over the hickey. I wasn't even sure who had left it.

He cleared his throat and put his hand out to help me off the bed. "You don't need to explain." He pulled me up and led me into the bathroom.

He turned on the water and then started unbuttoning his shirt. I hadn't seen him without his shirt on yet, and watched in anticipation. As the sleeves slid down his arms, I watched as his right arm came into view. Stunning portraits wrapped around his muscles; four smiling faces looked back at me. A woman. Twin boys about five. A baby girl.

I stepped forward as he started unbuttoning his pants and I slid a finger down his arm, feeling a lump form in my throat. His hands stilled on his belt buckle and he looked at his arm and then at me.

"My past life. I didn't want to forget what they looked like." He wiped a stray tear that had worked its way down my cheek before continuing to undress.

I had no words. His life was stolen from him and now all he had were the memories of what could have been. It had to be hard knowing they were probably still out there somewhere, at least his children, and he couldn't see them.

"Don't look so sad about it. Until Asher fell, he checked in on them from time to time. They grieved, moved on, lived their lives. That's all I wanted for them. To be happy." His eyes brightened and he slid my panties down my legs. "You know they say the best cure for a hangover is an orgasm."

I smiled back at him and climbed in the shower after him, the warm water falling over us and instantly making my tense muscles relax. "Who says that?"

"Me." He pulled me against him and kissed me, making my knees go weak.

The shower might have been small but my orgasm was not. Tobias was right. Orgasms really did help with hangovers.

OLIVER MORGAN. The celestial I still knew so little about. The boy who had fled after he and his friend had kissed. The boy who had decided that today he was sitting next to me in Demonology. You know, because I wasn't already confused enough as it was.

When he slid into the seat next to me, he said

nothing. He still said nothing when the whispers started. The whispers about why he was sitting next to me. The only angels that ever dared sit next to me were Brooklyn, Cora, and Ethan. I was beginning to think they were a special breed of angel.

Tobias cleared his throat at the front of the room and the class went silent. Despite his quiet nature, Tobias's presence commanded attention.

"Dean Whittaker has asked me to speak to you about recent attempted abductions of angels in Pasadena." The room erupted in chatter and he held up his hands to quiet the class back down. "As far as we know, there have been three attempted abductions. No angels have been reported missing yet, but as you know, some have assignments that require them to go off the radar. Dean Whittaker is asking you to stay on campus, and if you must go into the city, go in a large group. The Fallen seem to be attacking in groups of three."

"The Fallen aren't strong enough to abduct an angel," a girl in the back of the room commented. "Plus, we can just fly away."

Tobias's eyes briefly looked in my direction before he paced once in front of the room with his hand rubbing his bearded chin. "They are using demon blood, which weakens our defenses. Your wings won't work. You'll be too weak to fly or fight back."

"Then we attack the Fallen first," another boy

said, and the class bubbled up with noises of affirmation and agreement.

I don't know why but I clutched Oliver's leg under the table and he put his hand on mine. My mind had gone to Asher. Not all Fallen were abducting angels, and if angels went on a manhunt, innocent Fallen would be hurt in the process.

"I bet Danica is in on it." I flinched as the words hit my ears and Oliver's hand tightened on top of mine. "She gets here and now we have Fallen trying to kidnap angels using demon blood? The Princess of Hell is probably their ring leader."

"That's enough!" Tobias's voice was sharp and angry. The room fell silent once more. "Danica is not behind this. They attacked her."

"She rescued me and Levi last night." Oliver didn't turn, but spoke loud enough for everyone to hear. The room was silent. I didn't turn to gauge their reactions.

"If you have any other questions or concerns you can speak to me after class." Tobias spoke with finality and then started his lesson.

I tried to concentrate on what he was lecturing about, but couldn't keep my mind off of the Fallen and the three men slowly worming their way into my heart.

I WONDERED if I was still in high school or at a

guardian angel training academy. They were making up for the experience now, considering most of the angels here had missed high school. The stares and whispers were relentless.

When lunch rolled around, I was in a foul mood. My mood only got worse when Oliver sat down next to me. The air at the table disappeared as Brooklyn, Cora, and Ethan sucked in breaths and held them. I'm sure they had heard about the rescue and his presence at my side in Demonology, but seeing it was shocking after the events of the previous week. The other members of the Divine 7 were shooting daggers my way, even Levi. He wasn't shooting daggers when he had his tongue down my throat last night.

"Why are you sitting here?" I crammed chips in my mouth to keep myself from saying anything else.

Oliver glanced in my direction before sniffing at his sandwich and then taking a bite. He certainly was an odd duck. A cute, odd duck.

"I'm done being Divine," he said with a shrug. "Can I not sit here?"

A sound came from across the table but I kept my attention on Oliver. I narrowed my eyes. "You can't just undo what you've done to me."

"I'm aware of that, but I can at least try to make it up to you." He grabbed a cookie from a stack of five on his plate and offered it to me. "For you. I know you like them."

Brooklyn let out a snort. "So generous of you to

give her one. What are you, the cookie monster?" She looked at the cookies he had stacked on his plate. They weren't small cookies either, they were the kind you buy at a cookie shop. No wonder he smelled like chocolate chip cookies.

"Who's that?" he asked as I took the cookie from him and put it on my plate.

"The blue monster on *Sesame Street*... you know... C is for cookie, that's good enough for me, oh cookie, cookie, cookie starts with C." Brooklyn impersonated the Cookie Monster causing me to almost choke on the food in my mouth.

"Huh. That sounds like an interesting show. I'll have to check it out sometime." He grabbed one of the giant cookies and shoved half of it in his mouth, causing us all to laugh. He looked so serious about it that I couldn't quite tell if he was joking.

Ethan narrowed his eyes at Oliver and then leaned back in his chair with his arms crossed. "How do we know we can trust you?"

Oliver put down the other half of the cookie and folded his hands on the table. "I'm pretty good at keeping secrets, right, Danica?" He looked over at me with raised eyebrows.

My smile faded and I stared back at Oliver for a moment before clearing my throat and looking at Ethan. I knew he was referring to Tobias.

"He can be trusted. I wouldn't go telling him your deepest darkest secrets or anything like that."

After a few minutes of tense silence at the table, Oliver spoke. "Before dinner tonight some of us are playing a pick-up game of football with the staff. You guys should come and watch us kick their butts."

Cora made a squealing noise and perked up. "We should go. You haven't had one in forever!" She turned to me. "It's eye candy central! They usually take their shirts off, and let me tell you... Coach Ferguson and Mr. Armstrong are scrumptious."

"Sitting right here, Cora." Ethan laughed as he took a bite of his food.

I looked back and forth between them. Why hadn't I noticed the way they always sat so close to each other?

IT SEEMED like the whole school turned out for the game. There were no bleachers because the angel version of football was played in the sky. The field was twice the size of a standard football field. When the players took the field they were already shirtless with their wings out.

The first thing I noticed was that most of the male staff members were incredibly attractive without shirts on. Was that a prerequisite for becoming a guardian angel? Or maybe it was just that washboard abs were necessary to play football.

Tobias with his wings out gave me the female equivalent of a boner.

"Most of the women here are here for the show. It's like *Magic Mike* meets angels," Cora explained as we spread out a blanket and sat down. "They get pretty aggressive too since angels heal and all."

"I'm interested to see what happens with Oliver since he is now on team Danica and not team Divine. I bet they let him get pummeled by the staff, and you know how the staff like to go after Oliver since he's an archangel and all." Ethan sat next to Cora and pulled her close to him, putting his arm around her.

A pang of jealousy shot through me at seeing them cuddled up with each other. I wasn't typically a jealous person, but I wanted what they had. Someone to cuddle with openly and not just in clandestine moments.

A whistle blew and the angels shot into the sky. The student team included the five male Divine 7 and six others, in possession of the football. It appeared to be played very similar to actual football, but the tackles were in the air and much more violent. I cringed as the first student took a hit from Coach Ferguson, sending both of them onto the grass.

The rest of the quarter, which was shortened from a regulation game, was much of the same. The staff ended up leading three goals to two when the angels descended to take a break. Oliver made his way over to us, looking just as refreshed as when he had started. He had taken some pretty serious hits too, but since angels didn't sweat and they healed, he didn't seem fazed.

"How are you liking it so far?" He plopped down next to me on the blanket on his side and looked up at me. "Think I have a career in football?"

My eyes slid down his chest and abs to where his shorts rode low on his hips. It was almost a sin with how attractive he had been made. He was like a juicy cherry just waiting to be popped.

"It's fun to watch. You might have a career in male exotic dancing though." I bit my lip to keep myself from laughing when his face went from confused to flirtatious.

"You know, I'm a pretty good dancer. I should show you my moves sometime."

"Please make sure to do that in the privacy of your own room," Ethan groaned, throwing an empty water bottle at Oliver.

"Incoming," Brooklyn warned under her breath.

The rest of the Divine were headed in our direction as if on a mission. They walked with purpose, and at the front of their little group was Abby. They stopped a few feet from us. It was like a scene out of *Mean Girls*.

"May we help you?" I asked as casually as possible, trying to hide the fact that I wanted to jump up and beat the shit out of her smirking little face.

Abby ignored me and looked down at Oliver. "Oliver, this has to stop. You're embarrassing yourself being associated with this devil worshiper. We are concerned you're going to fall."

I snorted back a laugh and went to stand but Oliver put out his hand to stop me before he stood. He towered over the group with the next tallest being at least half a head shorter than him. He stepped forward and cleared his throat.

"You are a bitch." He spoke loud enough for every angel in the vicinity to hear and the whole area went quiet, which then in turn caused the entire field to turn their attention to the confrontation.

Abby made a noise in her throat and looked like she had been smacked but then a grin spread on her face.

"She fucked you, didn't she? Did her evil pussy put you under a spell? And here we thought you liked dick." The silence around us was deafening. It was one of those moments where I half expected a baby to start crying and snap everyone out of it. Everyone was holding their breaths.

Oliver took another step forward to get in her face but the four men of the group pulled her back and faced off with him. I stood up and grabbed Oliver's arm but he pulled it away from me.

Several staff members and Tobias landed next to us.

"What's going on here?" Tobias looked at Oliver and then at me.

"We were just getting Oliver so we could start playing again," Levi said.

"Well, let's go then!" Coach Ferguson jumped and flew into the air, the other players following him.

Oliver turned and gave me an apologetic look before following them. I stood facing Abby and Delilah.

"It's only a matter of time before he sees your evil ways, Eve. You better watch your back," Delilah spat as she and Abby backed away. They turned on their heels and took off into the crowd.

That certainly sounded like a threat.

Chapter Eleven

I had a gut feeling when I woke up Friday morning, Friday the thirteenth nonetheless, that the day was going to go badly. I'm not usually superstitious, but with life rearing its ugly head at me for no apparent reason, I couldn't help but wonder if it was karma biting me in the ass.

I woke up to no texts back from Asher. I had texted him every day since Tuesday, but my texts went unanswered, the silence speaking louder than words. I had thought something was there between us, but I was wrong. Tobias told me Asher was "complicated." Well, I could do without complicated in my life at the moment. Things were already complicated enough without a grown man not even bothering to text me back. Even a "stop texting me" or "leave me alone, stalker" would have sufficed.

Demonology had another pop quiz. Had I read

the syllabus like everyone else in the class, I would have known that every Friday there was a quiz so there really was no pop to it.

It was time for me to get my act together, buy a planner, maybe put things in my phone and set reminders. It was suggested to me before back in high school but I had never taken the time to actually do it. Maybe now was a good time to start. Tobias would help me if I asked. Ava would have helped me too, but I always felt I was already depending on her too much when she helped me with homework assignments.

Then there was glorified PE for pompous wing-toting beings, where I was reminded daily about my lack of wings. The rest of the class did warmups together, practiced drills, played games. Sometimes they didn't even use their wings, but I was banished to the room with the mats and the dummies.

"Do you think Coach Ferguson is going to let you keep me company the rest of the semester? Shouldn't you be learning whatever flying maneuvers the other angels are?" I asked Brooklyn, who was my constant companion the past two weeks.

We had just finished the drills we were running through and were stretching on the mats. I was getting better at throwing a punch and a kick, but still felt useless defending myself. Brooklyn told me it just took time and she had been even worse at the beginning of the year. She was good, easily connecting with her targets with an intensity I hadn't seen from another female before. If she got into a fight with a human male, she would kick his ass. That at least gave me a small sliver of hope.

"Actually, I think I found a solution to that. Levi is going to start training with me so I can keep training with you." A blush creeped up her cheeks as she turned away.

I thought she hated the Divine 7 just as much as the rest of us. Hell, I had thought I hated them too and now Oliver sat with us at lunch. Levi was a mystery to me after his abrupt mood swings. One second he seemed to hate me, the next to like me, then right back to hating me again.

"When did this happen?" I hadn't told anyone besides Tobias about my drunken night with Levi and Oliver. Since then, Levi had been avoiding me besides sending scowls my way, which I was actually grateful for. It would have been awkward being near him. What would we have discussed? Him using my nipple to make out with Oliver?

"Yesterday. Don't tell anyone, but we're going on a date on Saturday night! I know we aren't supposed to go off campus, but Levi says I will be safe with him." She spoke so surely, like she trusted him fully with her safety. I wasn't convinced.

"Levi almost got abducted on Tuesday. He didn't even put up much of a fight."

"I know. I told him we should just watch a movie here or something, but he says he isn't going to live in fear. He does have a point. We can't just sequester ourselves here on campus."

I studied the excitement on her face for several long seconds before getting up from the mats. I was surprised Levi would even want to go off campus so soon after almost being abducted.

"Just be careful. No dark, empty places."

"Yes, mom. What are you up to this weekend?" We headed towards the locker room where the rest of the class was already headed. "Are you going to see your mystery man again?"

Which mystery man was she referring to? I had three. Well, two now. "Maybe." I smiled to myself. Tobias and I had been seeing a *lot* of each other the past few days. I was still being overly cautious with Oliver and only sitting with him at lunch and in class.

We grabbed our clothes out of our lockers and I headed to one of the few showers that were in the locker room. Unlike my angel counterparts, I had to rinse off. They never sweated. Lucky bastards.

After getting dressed in my uniform, I went back to my locker to grab my bag.

"Oh my God! There's a snake!" A girl screeched, causing everyone to scream and start pushing and shoving to get out of the room.

At first I thought they were just being their normal bitchy selves and calling me a snake, but there was a literal snake in the middle of the locker room. I rolled my eyes at the chaos that erupted around me, grabbing my bag out of my gym locker.

I could have just left like the rest of them and let someone else deal with it, but the poor snake was a semi-harmless gopher snake. It was not happy with all the thundering feet, slamming lockers, and screaming girls. I could hear its hiss echoing as the locker room emptied. Gopher snakes sounded very similar to rattlesnakes when they were threatened.

"Well, buddy, looks like it's just me and you now. How'd you get in here? Please don't tell me you came from under the sinks." I got closer to the snake; his body was coiled and his head was up, assessing the threat in front of him, forked tongue tasting the air.

I could see how everyone had freaked out. He was massive and even looked very similar to a rattlesnake. Somehow, he had found himself right smack dab in the middle of the women's locker room.

I stood still until the hissing stopped and the snake started to slither out of its coiled position. Placing my hand on it about halfway, it stiffened and stilled under my hand, lifting its head again and tasting the air with its forked tongue. I waited for it to soften its muscles and start to move again. I very slowly picked it up, bringing my other hand up to support its body. It wasn't my first encounter with a snake.

"Poor guy... or gal." Since I didn't have anything

to put the snake in and I was not going to sacrifice my bag, I walked back into the gym, hoping to put it outside the gym door.

Dean Whittaker and Coach Ferguson were walking quickly across the gym towards me. The dean's high heels echoed their click-clacking sounds across the large room. The dean stopped several feet from me but Coach Ferguson had no qualms about the snake in my hands.

"What the hell is wrong with you?" His voice was raised and his hands were on his hips. "Bringing a snake into school!"

I continued walking towards the gym door because the last thing I needed was for him to be yelling in my face with an agitated snake in my hands. I stepped outside into the bright sunlight and set the snake down in the grass, letting it slither out of my hands.

"Danica, you need to come with us immediately," Dean Whittaker's voice projected from the gym door, where she and Coach Ferguson stood waiting for me.

"You can't be serious." I turned around and held my hands out in disbelief. "I didn't bring that snake in the locker room!"

"We have several trustworthy witnesses that say you did. Unfortunately, you are out of chances."

Two weeks. That had to be a new record for getting kicked out of a school.

IT WAS different sitting in Dean Whittaker's office this time, knowing I had done nothing wrong. They had called Tobias and we were waiting for him to arrive after his class. How could I, the daughter of the devil, really expect to come out ahead in this situation? The dean was never going to take my word over the word of a group of angels.

When Tobias entered the dean's office, I turned and watched him approach the empty chair. He didn't meet my eyes, but his neck muscles were tense. At least one of the staff members at this god-forsaken academy was in my corner.

"What's this about, Sue?" he said as he sat down next to me.

"I knew we should have never agreed to let such a loose cannon into this school and today she proved us right. She brought a rattlesnake into the women's locker room and let it loose. Someone could have been bitten!" She tapped a pen on her desk before setting it down. "I've already put a call in to the high court to decide if she should stay."

Tobias gripped the wooden arm of the chair and worked his jaw. He turned his head in my direction. "Did you take a rattlesnake into the locker room?"

I met his eyes. "First off, it was a gopher snake, completely harmless unless agitated. And no. I took it out of the locker room. It was there when I got done showering."

He turned back to look at the dean and cleared his throat. "With all due respect, I find it highly unlikely Danica would do something like this. How would she have even had the time to go and find the snake? She certainly didn't have it during her first class with me."

Dean Whittaker looked surprised and picked up a folder before dropping it on the desk edge in front of Tobias. "She has only been in attendance for two weeks and there have been countless reports and incidents involving her. Not to mention her history at her past schools. Now, I understand that Chamuel has a soft spot for Lucifer, but I've contacted Michael and he agrees that the high court needs to decide what to do with her. She doesn't show any signs of being anything other than a troubled human teenager."

In that moment, I wanted to scream. I wanted to stand up and take that folder and smack Dean Whittaker over the head. I would have if Tobias hadn't scooted his shoe over to touch mine.

"I see where you're coming from, Sue, but are you really that blind that you can't see what's going on right in front of your eyes?" My head jerked over to look at Tobias. "You allow the top angels, which are only top because of some ridiculous point system, rule this school and cloud your better judgement."

Dean Whittaker was very quiet as she stared at Tobias with a look of pure venom. Hell, I was even surprised Tobias had told her that, not that she didn't deserve his words because she most certainly did.

She finally spoke with no emotion in her voice. "Mr. Armstrong, need I remind you what happens to angels that go against the higher authority?" He shook his head, his body tense. "Very good. Her hearing is tomorrow at ten in the morning. You will go as her representative since she is unable to. Now, if you'll excuse me, I have somewhere to be."

She stood and walked out of the office, leaving us. I stood, grabbing my bag and throwing it over my shoulder. I was struggling to keep my emotions from bubbling over into a flood, but a stray tear managed to sneak out.

"Dan-" I put my hand up to stop him. He stood and took a step towards me, pain in his eyes.

I understood, I did. He cared about me, but it didn't change the fact that I wasn't an angel. I couldn't even go stand up for myself at my own hearing because I wasn't dead and couldn't go to heaven. Even if I could go plead my case, they would kick me out, I was sure of it.

"I'm just going to go start packing. I can take a hint when I'm not wanted, and I'm pretty sure this goes far beyond a hint." I left before he could stop me.

I kept my head down, going back to my room.

Never had I walked with my eyes on the ground, but sometimes hiding was better than having to look at stares and looks of disgust.

I couldn't help myself, I texted Asher once I was back in my room. *They are sending Tobias tomorrow to the high court to decide my fate. Maybe I can work on your construction crew? I can't use a hammer, but you could teach me.*

He didn't respond, which I didn't expect him to since he worked. I needed to talk to someone to keep the weight that was sitting on my chest from crashing down on me, so I called Lucifer. When he answered I couldn't even talk through the sudden tears that burst from me. I rarely cried in front of him, but I guess everyone has their breaking point. After several minutes of me crying and him staying silent on the other end, I finally was able to speak and told him about the snake and about the hearing.

"Mr. Armstrong will be going in my place since-"

"I'm coming," he stated firmly, but also with a hint of sadness in his voice.

"What? You can't come. Fallen can't get past the wards or go to heaven." I was sure he was aware of that small detail.

"I'll call in a few favors. I will see you tomorrow for breakfast."

He ended the call before I could even respond. The devil was coming to breakfast.

I PACED in front of the futon where Tobias was sitting. He was adamant that he would still be going, even if my dad had it in his head that he was going to somehow be allowed to go to the heavenly realm.

I had been mad at my dad for over two weeks, but for him to come and stand up for me in a place where he wasn't going to be received with warm hugs, it said a lot. He might have been an absent father but he always showed up when I needed him.

"Aren't you nervous?" I stopped in front of him and frowned. "I feel like you should be a little more nervous, like sweating through your shirt nervous. Need to take a cold shower nervous. You're going to meet my father. I told you he was the devil, didn't I?"

He laughed and crossed his ankle onto his knee. I didn't know if I was more nervous over my dad coming to campus, my possible expulsion, or Tobias meeting him. My dad had never met any of my boyfriends because I had never told him I had any. Not that any ever lasted longer than a few months. I had a feeling that what I had with Tobias was going to last a lot longer than that though so getting it out of the way might be a good idea.

"I don't sweat. I guess I'm a little nervous about meeting my girlfriend's dad, but it'll be fine."

"Girlfriend?" I smiled down at him, my stomach fluttering. "Is that what I am now?"

I walked towards him and lowered myself to straddle his lap, wrapping my arms around his neck. He groaned and buried his face in my hair, inhaling deeply, his hands moving to my ass and squeezing.

"Get your hands off my daughter."

If I was capable of jumping ten feet in the air, I would have. I hadn't even heard the door open or felt his presence. Yet there he was, Lucifer, standing just inside the door of my room. I nearly fell getting off of Tobias's lap, who looked just as embarrassed as I was.

"Dad, how did you get in here?" I turned towards him and plastered on a smile as if he hadn't just caught a man with his hands on my ass.

Tobias stood, stiff as a board. My father ignored me and gave Tobias the once over before giving me a hug. His firewood and cinnamon scent hit my nose and I buried my nose in his charcoal gray blazer, relief flooding me. He released me and his eyes were back on Tobias again.

"Sir, I'm Tobias Armstrong." I was impressed with his ability to introduce himself with a steady tone and stick out a calm hand for a handshake.

My dad took his hand and I swear I saw Tobias wince. My dad was probably doing something to him with his special voodoo tricks.

"Mr. Armstrong, is it? Care to tell me why a teacher is manhandling a student?" He let Tobias's hand go.

He walked around the room, looking in the cabinets, the refrigerator, out the window. We both watched him, unsure of how to answer that question. We had known it would come from someone eventually and that Tobias might face repercussions because of it. He finished his perusal of the room and turned back to Tobias, ignoring the look of horror on my face.

"Dad-"

"Let the boy speak, Danica." He looked at his watch and then back at Tobias.

"Well, sir, we, well, we..." he was stuttering, his forehead creasing with the struggle of how to answer the question. I had never seen him flustered or at a loss for words. He always spoke with confidence and strength.

Meeting parents was a big deal even under normal circumstances. These were not normal circumstances by any means. I had avoided this type of situation for years, my father never even having an inkling of my love life. If he only knew that there were two others besides Tobias. Well, one now that Asher seemed to have fallen off the face of the Earth.

My dad smirked, enjoying seeing him squirm. He slung his arm around his shoulder and moved towards the door. "Let's get breakfast and your *boyfriend* and I can get to know each other a little bit better."

"In the dining hall? Is that really a good idea?" I

followed them as he opened the door and walked into the hallway where two men stood waiting. They practically radiated power and had a faint glow to them, like someone had put lights under their skin. Oliver had a similar glow to him, just not as strong.

"Chamuel and Haniel will accompany us."

My eyes went wide as I took in the two archangels. They looked like normal men, just like my father, but you could tell there was an otherness about them. I just wanted to stare, but instead followed my dad, who still had his arm wrapped around Tobias like they were long-lost buddies. Poor Tobias; this had to be hell for him.

Walking to the dining hall, many students stopped to stare as we passed. They recognized Chamuel and Haniel, who my dad called Ham and Han, but they regarded my dad with curious glances and whispers. It was only a matter of time before they connected the dots that he was my father.

Once we got food, I made for my regular table, but my dad passed right by me and went to the corner seats at the Divine 7's table. I groaned internally and followed, sitting next to him on the far side of the table. I could try to explain to him that these seats belonged to a group, but instead tried to focus on saving Tobias from whatever my father had cooked up for him.

We ate in silence, but it didn't escape my notice

that the entire dining room was staring at us. Maybe it was the fact that there were two recognizable archangels eating pancakes at the other end of the table. Or maybe it was the sharp-dressed man sitting next to me. As far as I knew, no one knew Lucifer's actual appearance. At one point it was probably well known, but over the millennia it was twisted. He did somewhat look like Tom Ellis though, or was it that Tom Ellis looked like him?

"And who is this?" My inner dialogue was interrupted by my dad pointing a piece of bacon in the direction of Oliver, who was walking straight towards us with a large grin on his face.

He had no clue what he was about to walk into. I groaned and put my palm against my forehead. This was not going well. He already hated Tobias. Now he was going to meet the angel that had made it his mission to make up for his wrongs.

Oliver stopped and greeted the other two archangels before putting his tray down next to Tobias, leaning over the table, and kissing me on the cheek. Tobias chuckled as he sat down next to him.

"Good morning, beautiful. Why the long face?" He was much too excited for it being so early on a Saturday morning.

My eyes were drawn to his plate which was piled with cantaloupe and only cantaloupe. Since he had been eating with me, I had noticed he ate almost the exact same things.

When I didn't answer, he finally looked at my dad and then he smiled at him with the most welcoming and gracious smile I'd ever seen. It was endearing really, his complete obliviousness.

"I'm Olly." He looked down at the archangels who were watching him curiously. I couldn't tell if they were amused by him or not, but they both had a glimmer in their eyes. "You must have been created after I left?"

"I wasn't aware another archangel was created. When were you created?" He looked down at the piles of orange fruit on Oliver's plate. "Recently is my guess."

"July. What about you?"

I nearly choked on the soda in my mouth and my dad put his hand on my back to give it a few pats as I coughed. Oliver narrowed his eyes a bit at the hand on my back but didn't say anything. Oh God, he thought my dad was putting the moves on me. Gross.

"Long before that. So, tell me, how do you know Danica? Tobias here is her boyfriend, so who are you?"

Oliver looked at me and then at Tobias. He focused back on my dad's hand on my back. I didn't even want to imagine what was going through his head. Now that I knew he had only been *created* in July, he made so much more sense. He couldn't even recognize that two familiar archangels and Tobias being in the dining room was *odd*.

"I'm a close friend. And you are?"

"Just how close of a friend are we talking? Hands on her ass type of friend?"

I was going to die. Literally, I was going to die.

"Lucifer, leave the boy alone." Haniel warned from the end of the table.

Oliver's eyeballs nearly popped out of their sockets and he dropped his fork onto his tray. I gave him a reassuring smile, which didn't seem to help.

"We should get out of here before the Divine 6 come." I finished my last piece of bacon and piled my napkin and silverware onto my plate.

"What happened to the seventh one?" My dad turned slightly towards me with raised eyebrows, which was the most emotion I'd seen from him since he arrived. He probably somehow knew they sat at the table we were at and was biding his time to scare the shit out of them. Normally I'd be all for it, but it would only make matters worse. He *was* the reason they were such assholes.

"There is a seventh. They already replaced me with a second year named Betty." Oliver had a wistful look in his eyes but then cleared his throat. "Glad to be done with them."

The air suddenly changed at the table, taking on a prickling feeling of heat. My dad was no idiot. He knew the Divine 7 were my torturers and one was sitting right across from him at that very moment. The two angels at the end of the table put their forks down and looked ready to intervene if needed, but I shook my head at them. They may have known my father well at one point, but they didn't now.

Oliver's face turned a few shades shy of a tomato. "I... sir. I'm sorry. I just... It was funny at first, you know? You have to admit a room full of feathers is pretty hilarious. I didn't want to do the apple ball gag but... I will spend every remaining moment of my time here on Earth apologizing to your daughter."

"What. Ball. Gag."

I flinched and looked to Tobias for help. He was avoiding my gaze and was looking at the table. *Coward.*

"A prank. It was a stupid prank where they shoved a gag that looked like an apple in my mouth. I'm fine, Dad. Honestly. It's probably karma for all the shit I've done."

"Sir, I can assure you-" Oliver started, but Tobias reached over and squeezed the back of his neck.

"Just stop talking," Tobias said with a sigh.

Lucifer pointed his fork at Tobias. "I like this one." He then pointed his fork at Oliver. "This one. Well, no wonder they sent him to Earth."

Oliver's face fell at his words and before I could stop him he was rushing away from the table, leaving his uneaten pile of cantaloupe.

Chapter Twelve

$\mathcal{I}$ couldn't worry about what was going on with Oliver when my future lay on the chopping block. My dad struck a sore spot with the angel. It also didn't slip my mind that Tobias had mentioned knowing things about Oliver that he wouldn't want known. What had the angel done?

My thoughts of Oliver quickly vanished as we climbed the last set of stairs in Ariel Hall and exited onto the roof where we would be out of sight of curious eyes. I hadn't seen many roofs in my life, but this one had to be the cleanest roof in existence. It gleamed in the sunlight like a launch pad for the pure.

From what I had gleaned from the post-breakfast conversation, Chamuel and Haniel were taking responsibility for Lucifer through a sworn blood oath which gave them permission to kill him if anything went awry in heaven. When Haniel unsheathed a dagger that looked like it was encrusted purely in diamonds, I wasn't that surprised that all three of them sliced their hands and clasped them together.

"I'm not sure what state my wings are in. I stopped feeling them millennia ago." My dad took off his jacket, tie, and shirt, and handed them to me. He didn't wear clothing with slits for wings, since he couldn't use his. My heart ached knowing that my father was an angel, but couldn't access an essential part of who he was.

"Maybe when we're done, before we bind them again, we can have a quick race for old-time's sake." Haniel ran a hand between my father's shoulder blades as if he was searching for something. "This might hurt."

I clutched onto Tobias's hand as Haniel seemed to grab an invisible string and pull it away from my dad's shoulders before swiping the dagger through it. My dad fell to his knees, his back muscles scrunched. I was glad he wasn't facing me because I don't think I would have been able to handle whatever emotion was on his face. I took a step forward but Tobias pulled me back to him, shaking his head.

His hands fell to the smooth surface of the roof and his body seemed to vibrate with a power I couldn't understand. It was like a machine with a giant turbine was turned on, the waves radiating from him in a circular pattern.

"We should have done this in the field. It's going

to knock the entire building down!" Chamuel backed up a step.

The roof beneath our feet started to shake and Tobias pulled me closer to him. It felt like an earthquake, and I might have thought it was one if I didn't see my father's body vibrating in the middle of the roof.

Just when I thought my teeth were going to break from the vibrations, everything went eerily still and silent for the briefest moment and then wings burst from his back with a flash of bright light as he stood. They flapped twice, stirring the hair around my face.

I choked on a sob, the image of the man so hated, so vilified, standing before me with pure white wings that nearly blinded me. He turned around slowly, his wings moving as if on autopilot to avoid hitting Chamuel and Haniel. He walked towards me without hesitation.

"You've always wondered what my wings look like." He stopped in front of me, bringing a hand to my cheek and wiping away the tears that were cascading down.

His face looked different somehow. He was the same, but a lightness caressed his cheeks and he had a twinkle in his eyes. A sob escaped my lips and he pulled me into his arms, wrapping his arms and wings around me.

"Shhh." He kissed the top of my head and then

pulled away. "Everything is going to be fine. Shall we get this over with?"

He stepped back and Tobias followed him, giving my hand a squeeze as he passed. The four angels launched into the air and disappeared from sight.

~

WAITING for the angels to return was akin to going to the dentist. I hated it with every fiber of my being. They said it could be hours before returning, so instead of sitting around on the roof, I decided to track down Oliver.

I pulled my phone out of my back pocket and shot him a text. *Where are you? Want to wait with me?*

I was halfway back to my room when I got a response. I was thankful he hadn't pulled an Asher and ghosted me. *You can come to my room if you want. Building 2, room 403.*

Not exactly what I had in mind in terms of waiting, but after what happened in the dining hall, I couldn't really blame him for wanting to hide in his room. There were so many questions I had for him that, if I did have the balls to ask him, I wouldn't even know where to start.

He looked around twenty, yet was only about eight months old. He was at the top of the year one students, so it made no sense that he only had eight months of knowledge. Did he just pop into existence one day and already know a lot, or did he learn by sleeping with his head on books? I might hate him if he learned by osmosis.

Maybe I'd ask him why he wasn't in heaven anymore. That seemed rude though, and insensitive. So was asking him if he'd ever watched porn or masturbated. Did they have porn in heaven?

My mind was still going a mile a minute as I stepped out of the fourth-floor elevator of his building. I walked down the hall to his door, and before I could even raise my arm to knock, the door was opened.

"I felt you coming." He moved out of the way to let me in the room.

I stepped inside as he shut the door behind me and I looked around the room that was similar to mine, but decorated with blue accents. A large television was mounted to the wall in front of the futon, the Netflix logo displayed across it.

"You felt me coming? That's not creepy at all." I walked to the futon and flopped down, suddenly feeling exhausted.

He let out a small laugh and sat next to me instead of at the other end. "You can't feel us?"

I shook my head and nodded my chin towards the TV. "What are you watching?"

I reached for the controller on the coffee table and Oliver plucked it from my fingers before I could get into his account. His face turned slightly pink.

"Just some show. I was thinking of watching a DVD and then you texted."

"Liar. You were watching something sexy, weren't you?" I wiggled my eyebrows and giggled as his face turned even more pink.

Giggling was so out of character for me. I put my hand over my mouth to stop myself. I felt like I was a prepubescent teen with her first crush again.

"Don't be ashamed of it. Sex is natural. It's part of who we are." I grabbed the controller out of his hand. "And if you're watching something on Netflix with sex in it, then you need supervision, because who knows what misinformation you're getting."

"Sex isn't part of who I am. I was made out of thin air." He tried to grab the controller back but I moved it out of his reach. He let out a strangled sigh and crossed his arms.

I was so used to him being so jovial and smiling all the time that the downturned face and indifferent demeanor made something clench in my belly. I put my hand on his knee.

"The other night in Levi's room... sex *is* a part of who you are. A beautiful part of who you are."

"I didn't even like it though." He ran his hand over his face. "I mean I liked you, but then..."

"Then you kissed Levi." I searched his face, trying to figure out how he felt about kissing another guy. "How did that make you feel?"

"I didn't really feel anything." He put his hand over mine and squeezed it lightly. "Tobias told me only I would know what I liked. The shows I've been watching, it didn't seem to matter if it was a man or woman. I thought I felt something, but then Levi..."

"Sex is a funny thing like that. Sometimes we think something will turn us on and it doesn't, and then something will completely turn us on that we never expected. And what are you doing talking to Tobias about sex anyways?"

"He's my advisor. He's kind of like a big brother I guess you could say. I kind of feel bad always asking him stupid questions but he seems to know what he's doing."

"What do you mean by that?"

"Just that he's your boyfriend, and that one day that I walked in after you had, you know." He looked away at the red lettering bouncing around the screen.

"We were both stupid that day, and that's not why he and I are together. It's more than sex."

"What about that Fallen you were with on Tuesday?" He looked back at me, curiosity in his eyes.

"It's complicated, but he isn't even talking to me anymore. Like I said, sometimes you can't help what you like and don't like. If you like men, well, then you like men. If you like watching men having sex but only like having sex with women, then that's what you like. Don't think you have to fit any mold that you see on television or hear about from your friends. With that being said, how about we watch whatever it is you decided to enlighten yourself with and we can talk about it."

I pressed the button on the remote and the screensaver switched to the resume watching screen. I bit my lip, stifling back a laugh at the thought of him picking out *Sex Education,* thinking it was educational.

"I've been Googling things I'm confused about or texting Tobias to ask."

I was a little surprised about that but didn't say anything. "I'll be your Google. I've heard this show is pretty funny. Anything called *Sex Education* is probably not that educational if I'm being honest. Even if it was a show to teach you about sex, American sex education leaves a lot out, or makes you feel guilty for what turns you on."

He cleared his throat. "Do you have a lot of experience?"

I shrugged. "Probably average for my age. I mean, if you want to experiment on me, I wouldn't be opposed." I felt my face heat up with my words. Sometimes I just couldn't stop the words from tumbling out.

"I don't think I'm really ready yet. Plus, you have a boyfriend."

"Tobias says he doesn't care. I guess we'll find out soon enough."

"Soon enough?"

"Yeah." I patted his knee, leaving my hand there, and pressed the play button.

AFTER A FEW HOURS of watching Netflix and me answering way too many personal and nonpersonal questions about sex, Olly and I made our way back to the roof of Ariel Hall and sat against the wall surrounding the edge.

Hanging out with Olly was a good distraction from the nervousness that hit me like a Mack truck as we sat waiting on the roof. There had been a shift with me. Suddenly, I cared about staying in school and seeing it through.

Olly was naturally a curious person and had questions about everything, not just sex related. When he was created he was only given knowledge of heaven and a very basic knowledge of Earth and its history. He had absolutely no knowledge of the modern human world when he had started at Celestial Academy in the fall.

Whoever decided to send him to Earth didn't really consider how hard it was going to be on him. It was even worse than a prisoner rejoining society, especially since the Divine 7 had taken him under their dirty wings.

"Are you worried?" he asked, tracing a circle in my palm. I shut my eyes and put my head back against the wall.

"A little. I don't know why I care so much about this school. I've never been the school type." I had never enjoyed school, not because I didn't want to learn things or do something with my life, but because traditional teaching styles and the style I needed just didn't go hand in hand. Out of all the years spent in school, only two teachers understood my needs and really helped me.

"School is hard for you, isn't it?" I felt warmth radiating from the finger making a circle on my hand, causing my shoulders to relax.

I shrugged. "I have a hard time focusing, if you haven't noticed. I've tried everything. Pills don't work. Weed helped a little, but then again, it's illegal under twenty-one. Plus I don't really want to have to smoke something to focus long enough to read a page of a book."

"I have noticed the focus thing. I notice a lot." He moved his finger to my wrist and I bit back a whimper. Why did his touch have to feel so good?

"I've noticed. Thanks for the notebook and pen, by the way. It was thoughtful." I popped open an eye and looked at him; he was watching his finger move on my wrist.

"I'm sorry for being such a dick."

We sat in silence for a while before I put my head on his shoulder and nodded off.

I awoke to him shaking me gently. I rubbed my eyes and squinted towards the middle of the roof where the four angels stood in a circle, talking. I stood and walked towards them, silence falling over the group.

"Dad? How bad is it?"

"They're letting you stay," he said, turning towards me and letting out a sigh. He didn't seem happy.

"Just like that? They're letting me stay?" I was shocked. I was so sure they were going to kick my ass to the curb.

"We aren't at liberty to talk about what was discussed. Just know that you won't be going anywhere, but you need to at least try to stay out of trouble. The Divine 7 will be handled," Chamuel said as he and Haniel walked towards Olly. "Oliver, come with us."

"Sir," Tobias said, sticking out his hand to my dad. "Hopefully next time we meet it won't be under such circumstances."

My dad shook his hand and then turned towards me. "I need to get back. Try to stay out of trouble?"

I hugged him and handed him his clothing. He backed away, extended his wings, and launched off the building.

I turned to Tobias with my mouth gaping. "They let him keep his wings?"

"Something major happened in that room. Michael was there too. I wasn't allowed in, but when they came out they were quiet. You should have seen them on our way there though. It was like nothing I could have ever imagined. Laughing, joking with each other. It was like Lucifer had never left. The way back was pretty tense, but they wouldn't tell me what happened."

I frowned. I didn't like secrets being kept from me and that was certainly what was going on in this case. The question was, was it about me or the fact that Lucifer now had his angel wings back?

Chapter Thirteen

$\mathcal{S}$tudying. I hated it. There was nothing worse than staring at the pages of a book and trying to make sense of what it was trying to tell you. I had been neglecting my reading all week, and here it was a beautiful Saturday afternoon and I was spending it with my nose buried in a book.

Tobias was called into a meeting shortly after my dad left and I hadn't heard anything from him in hours. I was pretty sure it had to do with Olly, but there was also the slim possibility it was about me. I can't say I felt bad for him; he chose the wrong group to attach himself to. For all I knew, he could be putting on an act and I should tread carefully.

I stretched my arms over my head and swiveled back and forth in my desk chair. The sun had set at least an hour ago. How I had managed to study for as long as I had was a miracle. I stood and went to the kitchenette for my beverage of choice and a half-eaten bag of pretzels. I dumped a pile on my math notebook and plopped back in the chair. Getting my GED was probably the hardest thing of all. I sucked at math since I often got distracted in the middle of long equations and had to restart.

I grabbed my phone and propped my feet up on the desk. I pulled open the texts I had sent Asher and sighed. It was beyond frustrating. My thumb hovered over the call button. I hated talking on the phone but I longed to hear his voice.

Before I could chicken out, I pressed the button and brought my phone to my ear. One. Two. Three. Four. I moved the phone away from my ear on the fifth ring, ready to end the call, but Asher's voice brought it right back up.

"Hey." That was it. I should have been excited he actually picked up the phone, but my stomach clenched at his less than stellar 'hey.' He had been ignoring me for days and I had thought our hangout session had gone well. Or had it been a date?

I was at a loss for words. Me, Danica Marie Deville, at a loss for words.

"Danica? Are you going to say something or did you just call to be creepy as fuck?" In the background, I heard what sounded like pool balls hitting each other, and music.

Say something, you idiot. Instead, I hung up and threw my phone on my bed. I covered my face in embarrassment, despite no one being present to make fun of me. I *was* such a creeper. Who calls someone and just breathes into the phone? Serial killers, that's who.

I shoved a few pretzels in my mouth and let them sit for a second, the salt melting off and onto my tongue. I didn't like to play games, yet I felt like I was playing games with all three angels. Would they even be on board with me seeing all of them at the same time, or would they eventually make me choose? I *should* choose, yet I constantly thought about them, dreamed about them. How was that even possible? Did I even want it to be possible?

I pulled my feet off my desk and went to the bed. I stared at the phone and then picked it up again and hit the green button. This time he answered on the first ring. It was quiet in the background, like he had left wherever he had been.

"You're an asshole." The words left my lips before I could stop them. *Typical.*

He sighed into the phone. "I thought we had already determined that. Look, I've been busy and-"

"You could have texted me that. A simple 'I'm busy' or even 'fuck off.' Something is better than nothing. I thought we had a good time the other night." I laid back on my pillows and stared at the ceiling fan. I needed to dust the blades; they must have forgotten to clean them before I moved in. Or they didn't care they were dirty.

"We did up until you didn't listen to me. Do you

have any idea..." His voice trailed off and the phone went silent for a brief moment. I checked to make sure the call was still connected. "If you had been hurt or taken, that would have been on me."

"I'm not a child and I'm not going to apologize for following you."

"I didn't ask you to apologize. Besides that, it's too dangerous to be around me." He sounded dejected. I bet if I could have seen him, he would have been shoving his hand through his wavy locks.

I snorted. "Let me be the judge of that. Are you going to let me come over so we can finish our date?"

"Usually a date all happens on one day, not with four days in between. Is it really a good idea for you to come over?"

So, it was a date to him after all. It didn't slip my attention that he knew exactly how many days ago we had our date. It probably wasn't a good idea for me to go over to his place, but bad ideas never stopped me before.

"I can be there in about thirty minutes." My voice sounded hopeful.

He sighed. "If I don't answer, I'll be on the roof. Just let yourself in."

I couldn't stop the squeal that escaped my lips after hanging up with him. What the hell was happening to me?

I ENDED up stuck in Saturday night traffic and it took me almost an hour before I turned into the area Asher lived. He lived in an ideal spot, surrounded by buildings being revitalized and on a street that had come alive with restaurants and bars.

I pulled my car next to his truck and took several calming breaths before getting out. I really liked this guy, despite his smart mouth and avoidance of me.

I walked up the metal stairs to his door and knocked before trying the handle. He'd left it unlocked; I guess when you can snap necks so easily, keeping the door unlocked isn't an issue. I stepped inside, closing the door behind me and flipping the lock out of habit. The massive room was dark besides a small lamp near the bed and undercabinet lighting that reflected off the metal surface of the counters.

I set my purse on the table and walked through the empty room to the stairs leading to the roof. The only sound was the clink of my shoes on the steps and my thudding heart.

I walked onto the roof and smiled at the sight of him leaning on the rail, his forearms on the black metal. There was a small garden in one corner of the roof and a sitting area with a fire pit and a few chairs in another. There was also a hot tub with a gazebo covering it.

I approached him and cleared my throat. He didn't move from his spot, but turned his head to the side to acknowledge me before turning back towards the skyline. It was a beautiful view from the roof; part of the skyline lit up between the buildings and the fairly unpopulated area allowed just enough darkness to see the stars.

I stood next to him and leaned on the rail, my elbow brushing his. He looked over at me again, pushing his hair behind his ear when it fell in his face. I didn't speak, because I was at a loss for words again. He was a beautiful man. What do you say to someone you have such a deep yearning for?

Instead, he broke the silence. "When I was younger, before the war, I used to spend hours lying in the grass, staring up at the night sky." He ran a hand through his hair and then leaned his arms back on the railing. "I'd lie there for hours and wonder what was up there. I didn't think I'd actually find out one day. I didn't even believe in heaven." I put my hand on the crook of his elbow and squeezed gently. "I still remember the day FDR declared war. I was eating lunch at work and we were listening to the radio. We all left work and signed up to serve that same day. That was the moment when staring at the stars never felt the same."

I had watched my fair share of war movies, but had never really been around anyone who had gone to war. I couldn't even begin to wrap my head around what it was like or what it did to the mind.

"It's no excuse for me being an asshole. I can

stand here and try to tell you that I won't be an asshole again, but I can't promise you that. I'm messed up, Danica, and it'll be fine if you turn around and walk away." His jaw clenched and he gripped the railing.

I kept my hand on his elbow and let the sounds of the evening wash over us. A car alarm beeped in the distance and the faint sounds of music and laughter drifted from down the street. The soft whoosh of wings flew overhead as birds, or maybe they were bats or owls, flew towards the trees in the distance.

Once I felt I could trust my voice not to shake, I pushed off the railing and stood next to his hunched over body, turning towards him. I gently pulled on his elbow until he stood and faced me.

"I can handle you being an asshole, Asher. What I can't handle is you ignoring me. You have to use your words, or at least give me some indication that it's not me." I searched his eyes for an acknowledge-ment of my words. They sparkled in the faint light from a single strand of string lights wrapped around the edge of the gazebo and the faint sliver of moon. "Running from things doesn't make them any better."

He reached a hand up and brushed my hair behind my ear, his hand settling on my cheek. "I don't want to run when I'm around you."

My voice left me in a whisper. "Then stop running."

His lips captured mine as the final syllable left my lips. I leaned into him, and threaded my fingers through his hair. I could run my fingers through it all day and never tire of the silky texture. My tongue probed his lips, his mouth opening and our tongues colliding. He tasted like whiskey.

His tongue retreated and his lips moved to my neck, leaving a wet trail. The chill in the night air made me shiver as he tilted my head to the side, exposing the skin and trailing his lips over it. Scooping me into his arms, never breaking contact with my neck, my ear, my lips, he walked us back inside.

At the bottom of the stairs, he set me down and we backed towards the couch, or at least I think that was where he was leading me. I *hoped* that was where he was leading me. My nipples hardened in anticipation as he slid my jacket off my shoulders and it hit the concrete floor.

I started pulling up his shirt, which he grabbed from the back of his neck and yanked over his head. He pulled off my shirt next, letting out an appreciative grunt at the sight of my breasts covered in lace. We stopped moving when his legs hit the couch and I pushed him back, our breaths the only sounds in the room. It was like the room was in suspended animation, waiting for the clash of lips and our bodies to touch.

I lowered down on top of him, straddling his hips, my lips reconnecting with his in a bruising kiss.

He groaned as he gripped my hips and his fingers dug into them. I leaned forward, my lace bra and his naked chest connecting. His lips stilled and I was suddenly ejected from my seat on his lap onto the couch cushion next to us.

He sprang off the couch like a scorpion had pinched his ass and crossed to the other side of the coffee table, his back heaving with harsh inhales of breath. He didn't face me but his back muscles gave enough of a clue to know something was wrong.

"What did I do wrong?"

"Nothing. You did nothing wrong." His voice trembled with unspoken emotion. Unspoken pain.

I stood from the couch and reached for his fisted hand. He let me take it, and standing close behind him, but far enough to not crowd him, I peeled his fingers back and threaded my fingers with his. He let out a shaky breath, his shoulders relaxing little by little.

I put my forehead against his back and my head moved with his deep breaths. He was barely holding it together.

"What's wrong?"

"I don't deserve this. You." His voice cracked with his words and a sudden sob shook his body. "I can't keep feeling this way."

My chest clenched at his words, but I didn't speak. What could I say to that? That it would be okay? I didn't know him well enough to even fathom what was plaguing him. We all had our demons, and demons weren't defeated by standing idle and watching them do their damage. I placed my other hand gently on his back, hoping the light touch would at least give him some comfort.

We stood there like that for a while, with his sobs shaking us both. When they finally faded away, he turned to me, not bothering to hide the evidence of his tears. There was something so raw, so heart-breaking about seeing him like that.

It only made the desire to be close to him flare inside of me. I reached my hand up and wiped the tears from his cheeks, his eyes shutting at the gesture, a sigh escaping his lips.

"I'm sorry." He paused as if considering whether he should explain. "I get flashbacks."

"From the war?"

"That and the hours before my death." He kept his eyes shut. "You can't be on top of me."

"Is it okay if I hug you?" He nodded and I wrapped my arms around him, burying my face in his chest.

He let out a shaky breath. "I guess I ruined the moment, didn't I?" He chuckled and buried his face in my neck, his breath tickling my skin. "Thank you."

I ran my fingers up and down his spine before tracing his shoulder blade and the muscles under-neath. He moaned into my neck, his lips moving ever so slightly against the skin. I pulled away and grabbed his hand, leading him back to the couch.

I bit my lip and reached behind me, letting my bra fall from my shoulders. His eyes widened slightly as he appraised my breasts, taking in the smooth skin and pebbled nipples.

"You didn't ruin the moment." I grabbed his hand again and brought it to my breast, closing my eyes.

His rough thumb swiped over my nipple, the sensation making my core clench. He stepped forward, moving his hands to my hips, and kissed me, working his tongue between my lips. Whatever had happened a few minutes ago seemed to float away and now I was his sole focus.

His hands trailed to the button on my jeans, and in one flick he had them open and slid them down my hips, trailing kisses down my body as the fabric made its slow descent.

He stopped and pulled off my shoes before kissing my inner thighs while sliding the jeans off the rest of the way. It was a slow, torturous journey he was taking to get to the final destination between my legs. He slid his hands behind me and palmed my ass, kissing right above my slit. He was driving me mad, on his knees in front of me, kissing everywhere except where I needed him to be.

"You're a tease." I threaded my fingers in his hair and gave his head a little push.

He chuckled against my skin, the action vibrating and pulling a moan from my throat. He finally slid off my panties before standing and capturing my mouth again, nipping and sucking at my lips. One of his hands kneaded my breast while the other sat just to the side of my pussy, rubbing in a circle.

"Wait until I get you tied up to my bed. I'll remember you called me a tease."

His index finger trailed along my slit. I could feel my wetness taking over, begging to be used. His lips went to my ear, biting and nibbling as he slowly worked his finger back and forth. I moved my hips and he adjusted, just barely teasing the folds.

"Would you like that?" His tongue flicked my ear and I went weak in the knees. "I think you would." He slid two fingers into me, burying them as far as he could before curling them and slowly moving them left to right.

I didn't know what the hell was happening, but when he hit what he was searching for I gasped. He smiled against my ear.

"Too much?" I nodded and his fingers began moving in and out of me.

My breaths came out louder as his fingers slid in and out, the anticipation of his next move almost too much. I unbuttoned his pants and pushed them down, freeing his cock. I grabbed the base of it before trailing a finger underneath it and rubbing the head with my thumb.

"Now who's the tease?" I breathed as his two fingers moved to my clit, sliding it between them before stepping away from me and grabbing two pillows off the couch.

Excitement stirred in my belly as he put them on the floor and pushed the coffee table out of the way. He grabbed my hips and moved me towards the couch, pushing me down to lay with my lower half hanging off the edge, my shoulders and upper back still on the couch. My legs quivered as he lowered to his knees in front of me, adjusting my legs. The head of his dick teased my opening, and in one swift movement, he was buried inside of me.

His hands massaged my breasts as he thrust in quick, deep movements. My orgasm was already building as he moved his thumb over my clit, his touch sending me over the edge. My muscles tightened and my legs tried closing but he pushed them back open as he moved faster and harder, small grunts escaping his lips.

As my orgasm ebbed, his thumb returned to my clit, working it into an oblivion as my entire body felt like it ignited. His dick filled me, moving in with quick thrusts of his hips. I cried out as another orgasm hit me, and with two more thrusts, took him with me for the ride.

"Well, fuck me," I managed to get out between breaths, scooting back on the couch.

"I just did. You already want more?" He laughed and stood before walking to the kitchen and grabbing a hand towel.

I watched with half-closed eyes as he cleaned himself and handed it to me.

"I'll never look at your couch the same way again." I stood on shaky legs and made my way to the bathroom.

After cleaning up, I returned to find him in a pair of boxer briefs, a beer in one hand and the remote control for the television in the other. I could see myself with him night after night, curled up next to him on the couch.

I pulled on my panties and bra as he watched. Then I sat next to him, stealing his beer and taking a drink.

"You spending the night?" he asked, taking the beer back from me.

"If you want me to. It's getting kind of late so I should go if not."

"Stay. I have a hard time sleeping next to some-one, but we can try." He examined the controller for a few seconds before pointing it at the television and turning it on. "If it doesn't work out, I can just sleep on the couch."

I put my hand on his leg and gave it a reas-suring squeeze. "Who said anything about sleeping?"

alling asleep together didn't work out. We tried, even tried pillows in between us, but he just couldn't get comfortable. I understood, but at the same time was slightly disappointed I didn't get to cuddle with him, especially after he had worked my body like he owned it.

Getting back to campus put a damper on my mood. I had so much studying to do and still wasn't sure what was going on with Oliver or what the meeting Tobias attended was about.

Was it even worth my time to stay at a school that trained me to be something I wasn't? I was essentially just a human, with no angelic abilities as far as I could tell. I didn't plan on dying any time in the near future, so what was the purpose of me staying somewhere I was hated?

I walked into the dining hall and was surprised to see Olly already sitting with Ethan and Cora at our table. I half expected him to be missing or even sitting back at the Divine 7's table without me there. After grabbing French toast, bacon, and a bowl of fruit, I joined them.

"Where's Brooklyn?" I asked, sliding in next to Oliver and glancing at his plate of cantaloupe. I needed to ask him about that. It couldn't be healthy to eat that much fruit every day, although it wasn't like he could die.

"She should be here. Remember we're supposed to go study after we eat?" Cora turned and looked over at the Divine's table and then turned back to me. "She had her date last night, but never answered my texts about how it went."

"She probably just overslept." I glanced over at Levi to see him with his arm slung around Betty's shoulders. What a douchebag player. "If she walks in and sees that, I hope she goes over there and punches him in the dick."

"He's a player," Olly said, putting his fork down. "That's the right word, isn't it? In the last week he's been with four different people in some way."

"I almost forgot that you have the inside scoop on their deepest darkest secrets," Ethan said and then motioned towards Olly's plate. "You've eaten that every morning for days. Isn't your stomach all messed up?"

"It tastes good. Why get something else and risk it tasting bad? I don't want to waste food," Olly said, taking a defensive tone.

"I'd probably eat a plate of bacon every day if I could, but then I'd probably..." I shut my mouth for once in my life. "Anyway, maybe when we're done we should go wake Brooklyn up."

"You were going to say die," Cora pointed out. "It's okay if you say it. We're long past when we died. We wouldn't have been sent here if we were still grieving our old lives."

It still didn't help me from feeling like an ass mentioning dying in front of angels that were essentially dead people.

"Does bacon kill people?" Olly looked at the two strips on my plate.

Ethan chuckled. "God, you're strange. Bacon in and of itself doesn't kill people."

After we finished, we headed to Brooklyn's room. We knocked several times but she didn't answer.

"Did you try calling her? Some people just don't like texting." I knew this wasn't true since Brooklyn texted about anything and everything. I pulled out my phone and called her, the phone going straight to voicemail.

"Olly, maybe you can ask Levi if he knows where she is? I'm a little worried about her. She doesn't do things like this." Cora's brows pulled together in concentration. "Ethan and I will go check in the library, you two can talk to Levi and check in the gym."

We headed our separate ways. Olly called Levi

and he said he hadn't seen her since the night before when he dropped her off at her room. We walked across campus to the gym. She could have decided to practice her flying techniques since she was behind after helping me with hand to hand. The gym was empty.

Brooklyn was nowhere to be found and I couldn't help the fear that filled my gut.

BROOKLYN WAS MISSING and the rest of us were asked not to leave campus. Olly, Tobias, and I were sitting around Tobias's table.

"Do you think Levi is lying?" Tobias had a concerned look on his face. He knew both Brooklyn and Levi, but not enough to make any determination as to their character.

Olly shrugged. "He might be. You think he has something to do with her being missing?"

"I don't know but we can't just keep sitting here acting like she's not out there somewhere. She's not here on campus, so why aren't we out there looking for her?" I stood and walked to the window, pulling the curtain aside to look out. "Maybe Levi was a dick and left her in the city and she can't get back. What the hell?" I squinted through the window that had a reflection from the light in the room and then opened it so I could get a better view.

"What is it?" Tobias came up behind me and looked in the direction I was staring.

The same hooded figure I had seen before was sneaking towards the tree line before disappearing from view.

"I think that's the same person I saw the other night sneaking off." I let the curtain fall and turned back to the room, putting my hand on Tobias's chest. "We need to go to the city and look for her. We can call Asher to help."

"That guy scares me," Olly piped up, seriousness in his voice. He had only met Asher once and it had not been under the best circumstances.

I rolled my eyes. "Seriously?" I crossed my arms over my chest. "If you plan on hanging out anymore you are going to have to get used to him."

Tobias raised his eyebrows. "I thought he wasn't answering your texts."

With all the worry over Brooklyn, I hadn't had the time to talk to Tobias about Asher. "I went over there last night."

There. The Band-Aid was ripped off. Now I was officially dating two men at once. At least they already knew each other, although their relationship was strained.

"You went to the city? You know that we're supposed to-" Olly started.

"It's not like I was walking around. Besides, Asher clearly can kick ass. I'd be more worried about going to the city with just you two," I stated, smiling at them both.

"What's that supposed to mean?" Olly looked offended. He was the one who almost got himself abducted and there were two of them.

"She thinks we're weak because all she's seen us do so far is academics. I'll have you know that before Asher fell, I used to be right out there with him. I can throw a punch. I can kick some ass. Maybe if you're lucky, I'll kick Asher's ass so you can see just how skilled I am." He looked smug, but I was doubtful. I had seen Asher fight before. "So, you and Asher are what now exactly?"

I perched on the side of his bed and looked up at him. "I guess he's my boyfriend. And you're my other boyfriend. Is that going to be a problem?"

"You're wrong. I'm your boyfriend and he's your other boyfriend. And no it's not a problem, we talked about that already. I can't say I have any experience sharing a woman, but we probably need to all have a conversation at some point."

"Two boyfriends. Is that normal?" Olly stood and stretched, a small sliver of skin showing between his pants and shirt. I licked my lips because, good lord, was he attractive. It's like heaven decided to create the most beautiful male specimen to illicit impure thoughts.

"Normal depends on who you ask. It's not conventional, but I'm not a conventional gal now, am I?"

"Oliver, you were included in that conversation too." Tobias smirked as he watched me pick at a loose string on his quilt. It was old; I probably shouldn't have been picking at it.

"I was?" He sounded very excited over the prospect. I could feel his eyes on me. "You want to go on a date with me?"

I shrugged. "I'm drawn to you for whatever reason. There has to be some weird supernatural phenomenon going on, right? Or I'm just one horny woman. Makes sense considering my dad's the devil."

Tobias laughed at my joke, but the reference to the devil having horns went straight over Oliver's head, at least I think it did because he didn't laugh.

"I would have asked about it when we were in heaven, but your dad was right there and I really didn't want to get on his bad side. Remember, he likes *me*." Tobias almost sounded childish as he made reference to the breakfast from hell.

"At least I'm not her teacher." Olly mumbled it so quietly that I barely heard it, but it was out there nonetheless.

Tobias practically flew across the room, grabbed him by the throat, and shoved him against the door. "Listen, you little fucker, you don't get to judge people after the shit you've pulled. Or have you forgotten the reason you're here in the first place?" Tobias shoved into him one last time and then let him go. He dropped like a sack of flour to the floor.

"Care to elaborate on that?" I was standing now, ready to separate the two from ripping each other apart if necessary.

"Oliver, do you want to tell her or shall I?"

Olly sat against the wall and put his head in his hands looking dejected. It couldn't have been worse than the shit I'd pulled over the years, but then again, it probably did take a lot to get kicked out of heaven.

"It can't be that bad, can it? Just tell me. Remember who you're talking to here. No judgement from me."

"Oh, but this is so much more epic than any of the crap you got in trouble for," Tobias said.

"Shut up, Tobias. Olly, what is it?" I squatted next to him and tried to pull his hands away from his face.

He sighed and dropped his hands. "I broke into the artifact room and took the Holy Grail."

I bit my lip to keep from laughing. I didn't know much about religious artifacts, but I was pretty sure the Holy Grail was a big deal. "And *why* would you do that Olly?"

He looked at the floor and mumbled something.

"What was that?" I felt like I was a mother talking to her four-year old who just broke a vase and wanted to blame it on the cat.

"I was bored and there was this rumor that it turned water to wine and I just wanted to test it out. I was tired of just flitting around up there doing nothing. So I took it, snuck to Earth to get some water and it slipped out of my grasp. I couldn't find it." He let out a shaky sigh. "They told me I was such an idiot and needed to wise up, so they sent me here to teach me a lesson."

"Wait, wait, wait." I stood from my squat and looked down at him. "You're telling me you lost the Holy Grail? How does that even happen?" Tobias was laughing now but was trying to cover it by covering his mouth. "Where were you trying to get water from?"

He looked to Tobias with a pleading look in his eyes, which only made him laugh harder. He rubbed his hands over his eyes and then looked at me again. "The Pacific Ocean."

"Don't stop there, Olly boy. Tell her the whole thing," Tobias choked out between laughs. I had never seen him laugh so hard. He had clearly heard this story before, but probably never heard it from Oliver's lips.

"Near Hawaii, I swooped down to scoop and a wave knocked me in. I dove after it but it sank so quickly and none of us could find it. It's lost forever. I don't know why they got so mad about it. I told them they can just go to the store and buy wine now. They don't need a cup that makes it."

I joined in the laughing now. "There are probably a lot of people that would love to get ahold of a cup that turns water into wine. I wonder if the ocean will eventually turn to wine."

"There is a bright side to my punishment though. At least here I get to talk to people and have fun. Plus, I get to talk about sex with you." He looked at me and then at Tobias and smirked. Maybe Olly wasn't completely oblivious after all.

Tobias stopped laughing. "You probably don't even know what hole to stick it in."

"Tobias! Seriously, how old are you, twelve?" I stood and pulled out my phone. "I'm calling Asher. He, at least, doesn't act like a child."

Tobias snorted. "Hate to break it to you, but Asher is ten times worse. You think his foul mouth is bad, wait until all three of us are vying for your attention at once."

I raised my eyebrows and then shrugged. If they wanted to act like petulant children around each other that was their own business.

WE PULLED up outside of Asher's place and I really just wanted to get out of the car. Maybe it was the stress of everything over the past several weeks, but my irritation was at an all-time high. Their bickering started the second we got to my car and Olly called shotgun. The entire drive I wanted to throttle them both. But then I also kept imagining myself ripping their clothes off and letting them both have their way with me.

I should have taken them up on their offer to *fly*

me to Asher's, but considering I was scared of heights, I declined. Instead, I was stuck in a not-so-large car with two testosterone filled males who were displaying their feathers like damn peacocks. Although, I suppose I was more of the peacock since I essentially had a harem and they were territorial like peahens.

"Is it safe to be here? It looks like one of those creepy buildings in a movie just before the heroine gets murdered with a giant knife," Olly commented as he slid out of the car. "Don't worry, Dani. I will protect you."

"What the hell have you been watching? You know all that crap is only partially based on reality, don't you?" Tobias retorted, slamming the door of my car shut which made me scowl at him. "You can't protect her. You'd probably slip and drop her."

"Can you two just knock it off?" I stomped up the stairs and banged on the door with my fist. I would normally find their banter funny and join in, but Brooklyn was missing and who knew how many other angels we hadn't been told about.

Asher opened the door with a confused look, probably at why I was banging instead of knocking. He looked behind me and then seemed to comprehend the reason and pulled me to him, kissing me on the lips. I let out a surprised squeal and leaned into his chest. Tobias cleared his throat.

"Oh, hey guys. Didn't see you there. Come on

in," Asher said, moving out of the way. Great. This was a really *great* idea.

Olly walked in behind me and looked around wide-eyed like a kid in a candy store. I wondered if he had ever been in a candy store. We needed to start a list. "This place is awesome!"

There was an awkward moment between Asher and Tobias as Tobias entered. They hesitated before Asher stuck out his hand and they shook. They were totally thinking about hugging.

"You brought the idiot from the other night?" Asher asked, watching Olly move into the place like he owned it. He picked up a wood carving off an accent table and examined it before Asher snatched it from his hands and put it back.

"Asher, be nice," Tobias warned. Funny words coming from someone who hadn't been so nice himself.

Olly took a step away from Asher and held up his hands in mock surrender before angling his body towards me. "Great, now both of your boyfriends are going to gang up on me. Maybe you and I should just ditch them and ride off into the sunset together. What do you say?"

"You can all either get along with each other or-" I bit my cheek to stop myself.

"Or what, Danica?" Tobias raised his eyebrows.

What I really wanted to say was that I would spank them, but held it in. For once I didn't want to add fuel to the fire. We had shit to do, and saying something about spanking probably would not help. Instead, I said, "Let's just get this over with. Where are we going to start?"

"The Fallen have been operating in places where there aren't a lot of people around. Park after nightfall, empty parking garage, empty alley. I doubt they'll go to the same place twice, at least not so soon afterward," Asher said, moving across the room and grabbing a laptop off his desk. He moved to the kitchen table with it. While it powered on he stood and went to the refrigerator to offer us drinks.

After pouring himself a glass of whiskey, he sat back down at his laptop and paused his fingers over his keyboard. He looked over his shoulder at Tobias, then turned to face him. "So, I need to tell you about something I did a few years ago before you see my background."

Tobias looked confused, but it was Olly who spoke. "It's okay if you have naked girls on your background, or hey, even naked men. You do you. You should see my computer background."

Asher's eyes snapped to Olly and narrowed slightly before moving back to Tobias. "As you know, as a Fallen no one really keeps an eye on what I do if I stay out of trouble, so I took a little trip to Philly when I heard that Margie died."

Tobias's hand gripped his beer bottle tighter, his knuckles turning white, and I hoped it wasn't going to break. Or that he wasn't about to hit Asher over the head with it. I looked between the two men, wondering if they were going to come to blows again. Olly noticed the tension radiating off of Tobias too and backed up a few steps. Tobias always had an air of calmness about him, so to see his hackles bristling was off-putting. It had become more and more frequent lately.

"She was ninety-nine, died in her sleep. Anyway, I approached Jeffrey and told him my great grand-father served with you."

Tobias took a really long gulp of beer, at least half the bottle. "Why are you just now telling me all of this?"

"Didn't quite know how to tell you. We got to talking and he said that Margie had given them a box of pictures shortly before she passed. He let me borrow them and I got them scanned. I have been waiting for a good time to contact you about them."

"You had no right to do that," Tobias ground out between gritted teeth. He walked to the kitchen window and looked out. "So what, you have my family plastered as your background?"

Asher typed in his password and logged in. "There were quite a few pictures of our platoon in the box. I did scan all of the photos though. I'll share the folder if you want."

Tobias walked back over to the table and I pulled Olly away to sit on the couch to give them privacy. There would be time later for us to look at pictures, but the two men needed a moment. Tobias was visibly tense, but then his shoulders dropped as

Asher said something and they both laughed. After a few minutes of hushed talking, Tobias turned with shining eyes and waved us over.

We gathered around Asher and watched as he pulled up a map. He zoomed in so that a mile radius was showing and pointed to the three known points of abduction.

"Why are the Fallen even taking angels?" Olly asked, then turned to me. "We should ask your dad. Maybe he might know something."

"You think my dad has something to do with this?"

"Well.. he is the OG fallen angel."

If he hadn't been talking about my father, I would have laughed.

"I think what Olly is trying to say is that at one point in time the Fallen thought they were meant to be his army, and since they are using demon blood, maybe there's something he might shed light on," Tobias said. "It's worth a try."

I stepped away from them and pulled up Face-Time on my phone. If I was going to ask him if he was kidnapping angels or supplying demon blood to the Fallen, I would at least do it to his face.

He answered without video and the first thing we heard was screaming. "Just a second." He put us on hold, the phone going silent.

"Was that seriously just a scream?" Olly looked at me with wide eyes. "Is he in hell right now torturing someone?"

"Don't freak out so much. He usually still answers even if he's in the middle of something." I shrugged because it wasn't that big of a deal. Well, maybe it was a little bit of a big deal.

"And you're okay with him torturing souls?" Olly seemed really concerned so I put a hand on his forearm. He looked down at it and then back at me.

"It's his job."

"His job was to let the souls exist in the after-world in isolation, not torture them."

"Not entirely my fault, boy," my father said. He must have come back on the line mid-conversation. "Danica, please tell me you aren't in trouble again. I'm getting too old for this."

I snorted back a laugh. "I'm not. My friend Brooklyn is missing and we are trying to figure out what the Fallen would want with angels and how they are getting demon blood."

"Who is there with you?" he asked and I told him. "So there are three men now? Is there a fourth? Figures Michael was only seventy-five percent accurate. The archangels are investigating this. You need to stay out of it, especially if Oliver is involved."

What. Did. He. Mean.

"Wait, a fourth? What do you mean Michael was right? You hate Michael. And what about Oliver?"

"Hate is a strong word. It's more of a strong aversion to him. Oliver isn't just a regular angel. He didn't ascend, he just *is*. Like me, Han, Ham, Michael. Any of us would probably be a major win for whatever they are up to. If they get their hands on him, that probably wouldn't go very well for him."

We all looked at each other. They almost *had* gotten their hands on him.

"What are they doing with angels, Dad?"

"We can't be sure, but we think they're using their blood. It only makes sense that's what they're doing. An angel's blood is a powerful catalyst for creation."

"What do you think they're creating?" Tobias asked.

"Whatever it is, it isn't good. I'm still interrogating all of my surface demons to see if they know where the demon blood is coming from. Demon blood has the opposite effect as angel blood."

"Wait, you have demons here on Earth? Isn't that against some kind of law?" Olly said, not realizing that he was continuing to dig himself into a hole with my father. If he wasn't careful he was going to end up at the same level of disdain as Michael.

My father laughed. "Son, if I didn't have demons dealing punishments on Earth, I'd end up with a whole hell of a lot more souls down here. When the guardians can't help the soul, I step in. I'm assuming they don't teach you that now, do they?"

"You don't have anything to do with this, do you?" I asked slowly, cautiously.

"Danica, I have angel blood myself. If I needed angel blood, I'd just use my own. Please, just... be careful. You have always had a faint angel aura about you and we don't know the composition of your blood, but it has to have some angel quality to it. If they took you and then found out you were mine..."

We ended the call after that, saying our good-byes, and I stared at the phone for a moment before looking at three sets of inquiring eyes. "We've never had my blood tested and I've never been to a regular doctor. He's paranoid they'd somehow find a way to take me and experiment. My dad pays for a private doctor or he just heals me himself."

We turned back to our map.

"There are way too many places to look," Asher said.

"What if we should be looking for where they're taking them," I piped in. "Where do the Fallen like to live?"

"Well, if they are off the rails, then abandoned buildings. That's how I found this place. Not far from here there are some empty warehouses." He looked back at the map, not seeming to notice that he just told us he was 'off the rails' at some point. Whatever that meant.

"We have to start somewhere. How are we

getting there?" I asked, not sure if I wanted to be stuck in my car with three men.

"Flying would be faster but someone is scared of heights. Funny considering she's half angel," Tobias joked, nudging me in the side with his elbow.

"Even if I did agree to fly, won't someone see us?"

"No. It's a short distance. It will be a good way to break you in. You can fly with me," Olly said.

Asher went to his closet and disappeared. He popped his head back out a few seconds later. "Toby, come get a gun." Asher disappeared again and Tobias went into the closet with him. They came back out, but both had bulges in their front pockets, and it wasn't from them being happy to see me.

"Do we not get guns?" Olly asked. I highly doubted Olly had even seen a gun up close before. He'd probably shoot his eye out.

"Do you know how to shoot a gun?" Asher asked.

"Well, no, but how hard can it be?" Olly replied, shrugging as if handling a firearm was no big deal. If he couldn't keep his grasp on a magical goblet, I would hate to see what happened if he fired a gun.

FLYING, even if just for a minute, was much

different than I expected. I thought I'd feel dread at the thought of plummeting to my death, but instead felt weightless and free. It also helped that I was wrapped in Olly's strong arms and could bury my face against his chest, the smell of cookies filling my nose. I was grateful he wasn't addicted to something like broccoli or asparagus.

We landed at the edge of a field filled with dead weeds and littered with trash. We quickly followed Asher and Tobias who had landed before us. I wished I had gotten a picture of Asher being carried by Tobias, but I heard that pictures of an angel with wings out came out blank.

"Won't they sense us or something if we get too close?" I whispered as we scooted along the side of a brick building with half of its windows busted out. My boots crunched on the broken shards of glass and debris littering the ground.

"Not with me here," Tobias said glancing back at me. He didn't elaborate and the look on his face told me he would tell me later. Knowing me, I'd probably forget to ask. I needed to spend some time in the library reading about angels because there was way more to them than just having a pair of wings.

As we walked, we looked in the windows of the building. It showed signs that, at some point, people had squatted in it, but it was currently lifeless besides the faint sound of scuttling feet on the concrete floor I could hear through the broken windows. Gross.

We moved around the side of the building to an access road where large tractor trailers could have access to loading docks. A chill ran up my spine as we made our way to the next building. I felt like something was going to jump out and attack us.

"This is like looking for a needle in a haystack. It's going to take forever to check all of these buildings. Can't we split up?" I felt restless, even though we were moving. The thought of having to look in each and every building was daunting.

"If we split up then two of us won't have Tobias's suppression skills," Olly explained.

"I can extend it, but every angel in the bubble will have it and they will notice when they can't sense each other."

"Unless they have an angel that can suppress too. I can't sense any angels in any of these buildings," Olly said, stopping and shutting his eyes.

We turned towards him, curiosity on our faces. He shook his head and opened his eyes again.

"How far can you do that and why didn't you mention anything before now?" Asher let out a heavy breath of air like he was trying to suppress the need to wring his neck.

He shrugged. "No one seemed interested in what I had to say. Besides, I really wanted to fly with Danica in my arms."

Tobias squeezed the bridge of his nose and

Asher started walking back the way we had just come. I felt bad for Olly and I was tempted to wrap my arms around him and tell him I was interested in what he had to say. Even if sometimes what he said was off by a mile.

"To answer your first question, I haven't really tried to see how far I can see. Michael is supposed to train me on how to use the sight fully."

"What is the sight? Is there an 'Angels for Dummies' book somewhere?" I was really feeling out of the loop. It was possible that I missed all of the information I needed to understand angels in the first semester of the year.

"I can focus on something and locate it. The location will flare in my mind. If I've been close to the person then I just know the little flare is them. Not sure how that works. That's how we found you last week. All angels have some sensing ability but it usually only expands a short distance."

"You could sense her from campus all the way here?"

"Yes."

"And you're just now telling us this."

Olly looked down and kicked at the ground. "What would I even look for? There are angels and Fallen all over the Los Angeles area. It's a giant speckled map of light."

"If you look for a large group of Fallen or even a few together... remember Fallen usually aren't with other Fallen," Asher suggested.

We were back at the edge of the field we had landed in and stood in a small semicircle around Olly. He shut his eyes and took a deep breath. I could see his eyes moving under his eyelids, like he was dreaming. What other special abilities did these angels have that I didn't know about?

"No large groups. There's a group of four Fallen moving in downtown like they're in a vehicle. No, wait. Three Fallen and an angel. It's..." He gasped and his eyes popped open. "We have to go! They have Levi."

He grabbed me and his wings extended. "Wait! You need to see where they go. If we go in there with guns blazing then we might not figure out where they're taking them," I said, pulling away from him.

"So we just *let* him get taken? That's ridic-"

"She's right. Plus, if he's stupid enough to get abducted twice, I have no problem using him as a sacrificial lamb," Asher said, putting his hand around my waist and pulling me to him.

Olly narrowed his eyes at Asher, for what seemed like the hundredth time, and then shut his eyes again. Asher drummed his fingers on my hip before sliding his hand in my back pocket and squeezing my ass. Tobias watched us and licked his bottom lip before turning his attention back to Olly.

Asher put his lips to my ear, his warm breath tickling my ear as he said, "He likes to watch."

My eyes went wide and I turned my head to

look at Asher, our faces inches apart. He glanced down at my lips and then lowered his to hover over mine.

"If you're interested in that kind of thing," he said.

"They vanished!" Olly said. I pushed away from the trance Asher had me in and tried to look innocent. "That must be where they're taking them, but I thought Fallen didn't have any of their abilities?"

All eyes went to Asher who said, "We don't."

"Let's go," Olly said, scooping me up, causing me to let out a small squeal.

Tobias picked up Asher the same way as he grumbled under his breath about feeling like a damsel in distress. I shut my eyes as we took off from the ground. I was still too scared to watch but as soon as we were in the air, it felt like we were in a pneumatic tube, like in the bank drive-thru.

We landed softly and my feet touched the ground. I blinked my eyes open and stared up at a five-story white building with a domed roof in the center, a cross reaching into the night sky. Chills ran up my arms and I rubbed them through my leather jacket.

"What is this place?"

"It's an abandoned hospital," Tobias said, taking my hand as we jogged to the building to stay out of plain sight. "What's the plan?" He looked at Asher.

"Figure out what they're doing, how many angels they have. No heroics, at least not tonight."

Asher looked at me and then at Olly. "No matter who or what you might see. There are going to be more than just three Fallen in there."

"Let's split up. Now, I know you aren't going to like this, Asher, but you and Olly pair up. I'll be with Danica. That way there's experience plus someone with wings."

Asher grumbled something under his breath but then nodded.

"Let's do this." I tried to sound confident but wasn't so sure.

Chapter Fifteen

Oliver

*A*sher Thorne. His last name fit him to a T because one thing was for certain, he was a thorn in my side. Not only was he Fallen but he also looked at and touched Danica like she was a piece of meat.

They both did. Tobias and Asher were predators and she was their prey. When I had walked in after she and Tobias had done who knows what on his desk, it took everything in me not to sling her over my shoulder and get her away from him. I may have been naive and inexperienced, but having sex on a desk, in a classroom, is no way to treat a lady of her caliber.

Too bad Tobias knows too much. Could you imagine if it got out that I lost the Holy Grail?

Everyone already laughs at me because I'm quirky. Yeah, we'll go with that. I'm a quirky guy.

It was Tobias's idea to split up to check out the abandoned hospital that probably had ghosts. Or zombies. Or a nest of vampires. Or the Gargoyle King. I wasn't nervous, not one bit. I could take on any of those.

I followed Asher just far enough away from him to be out of reach. We did not get along and I wouldn't put it past him to choke me or snap my neck. Neither of those would kill me, but they wouldn't feel pleasant.

As we moved around the front of the hospital we looked in windows and saw nothing except the faint glow of exit signs and a few dim lights running down the length of the hallways. Why did it still have power?

"It still has power," I commented.

"Thank you, Captain Obvious."

God, he was such an asshole. What Danica saw in him was beyond my comprehension. Well, maybe not completely beyond my comprehension. He wasn't ugly, at least on the outside. Also, it seemed, at least from what I had watched, that women seemed to forgive a man for being an asshole if he had abs and a big dick. Asher probably had the biggest dick known to man to make up for how much of an asshole he was.

Why was I thinking about Asher's dick?

We rounded the side of the building and ended

up in a partially closed off area. Parked in a neat row were five gray vans, the same as the one that had tried to take me. Asher put his arm out and stopped me from moving forward and we moved behind a dumpster. He pulled out his phone and sent a text to Tobias.

What we needed were walkie talkies or those ear communication devices the secret service used. I would want my name to be Golden Cherub. It has a nice ring to it.

"We need to find a way in. Stay close." He crouched down and I rolled my eyes at his back before following him.

I didn't really agree with this plan of theirs, to just check things out. Levi was in there, and probably Brooklyn too. We needed to act fast. Angels couldn't exactly die again, so whatever was going on with them was something I didn't even want to think about, but I couldn't help it. Was it like a torture chamber in there? I shuddered. Danica was right; I needed to stop watching so much on television.

Asher stopped at a window and tried it. Locked. I shoved him out of the way and put my hand near the lock and then slid the window open.

"Wipe that smug look off your face, angel baby." Asher moved me out of the way with his shoulder and climbed through the window first.

I followed and resisted the urge to slam him against the wall. That would make too much noise.

He opened the door leading out of the abandoned office we were in and peeked out.

"You are damn lucky they didn't get you and your friends the other night." I knew it was only a matter of time before he yet again made me feel like a complete fool. I knew I was lucky, both me and Levi. If Asher hadn't rescued us, I would probably be living out a real-life horror movie. Except now, Levi was.

"That stupid idiot. He can't even go two days without checking in on his record. I bet that's why he was in the city."

"What do you mean?" Asher turned back to look at me.

"He has the top score for some arcade game in the mall. He's obsessed with it."

Asher's frown deepened as he studied my face. He then made a gesture with his head for me to follow. It wasn't like I could argue with him. We crept down the hall, the silence in the abandoned halls deafening. We stepped lightly, trying to keep the sounds of our footsteps to a minimum. There were so many hallways it was going to be difficult to remember where we came in, if that even mattered. Asher cut across a large open area that looked like a former emergency room and started going up the stairs.

"Is that a good idea?" I whisper screamed. They could come down at any minute.

He shrugged but continued up, with me hot on

his heels. I might be safe from dying, but Fallen could die. Did this guy have some kind of death wish? Fallen lost their wings, their healing ability, and their sanity.

We reached the top of the stairs and Asher grabbed my arm and yanked me behind a large desk in a crouch. The faint sounds of voices came from down a corridor, but we were still too far away to see what was going on or to hear what they were saying.

He pulled out his phone again and texted Tobias, then we were on the move down the hall, ducking in a few rooms to make sure no one was coming. If I could sweat, I'm sure I'd have been sweating bullets. We made it to the last room before a large open area and Asher put his index finger over his lips.

Did he think I was a complete idiot and was going to talk? He crouched low again and we darted behind another large circular desk and then into a dark storage room. We couldn't see much, but could see the backs of a few men.

"Any problems tonight?"

"None. The kid says the academy has told the students to stay on campus. He was able to get us that sweet little thing last night, but tonight we were unsuccessful. Maybe we should go back to finding guardians."

"The guardians suppress their signatures most of the time, that's why we switched to the academy punks. When do you twerps learn suppression? Back in my day they didn't have a fancy training academy."

"Third year."

My eyes went wide at the sound of Levi's voice and Asher's eyes met mine. He shook his head at me and then turned back to watch out the door.

"She says we're taking too long. We need to recruit more. After those nine were killed, we need all the help we can get. The last thing we want to do is piss *her* off."

I was about to mouth something to Asher when the sound of squeaky wheels and weeping drew my attention back to the large open room. Judging from the signs still hanging on the walls, it was the holding room for the operation room.

I strained to see and caught a glimpse of a rolling cage of sorts and a head of brown curly hair that was tangled but sat in a distinctive bun on the top of her head. I was so focused on looking that I didn't notice my foot was right next to a fire extinguisher on the floor. When I moved back, my leg knocked it over, the clang of metal on linoleum loud in the mostly silent emptiness.

"Who's there?" Quick footsteps made their way towards our hiding spot, but there was nowhere to go.

My wings extended, quickly folding forward and grabbing Asher. I moved us toward the back of the storage room, Asher tripping over something in his backwards movement, sending us falling to the floor.

"Wha-" I put my hand over his mouth and shook my head, pleading with my eyes for him to stay quiet. He tried moving out from underneath me, but I had several inches on him, plus my wings helped hold him still.

It was dark, but I could make out the white of Asher's wide eyes before they clenched shut and his body trembled underneath mine. What the hell was he so scared for? He could snap necks like it was his job.

A light flicked on overhead and I breathed slow, even breaths as a few sets of heavy shoes walked into the room. Someone moved the fire extinguisher.

"Maybe it was a ghost."

"They do say this place is haunted. I don't see anything. Let's go."

The light was flicked off and the footsteps retreated but the men stopped outside the door to talk with two other men. Asher continued to shake. Moisture soaked into the side of my hand, which was still against his mouth. I wanted to take my hand away but knew that would be a bad idea.

I heard the men move a little farther away, but not far enough for comfort.

I lowered my mouth next to his ear and whispered, "Are you okay?" He shook his head. "I can help but I need to move my hand off your mouth. Can you stay quiet?"

One of his hands clutched the back of my shirt. He nodded. I took my hand off his mouth, ready to put it back if he made any noise. I placed my hands on his cheeks; the wetness felt like tears. I wiped them away with my thumbs.

I could feel his heart hammering into my chest. I'd only tried this once with Abby when she had a memory from her past and freaked out. I hadn't even known what I was doing at the time, but when I had grabbed her face in my hands to get her to stop screaming, she calmed.

I stroked Asher's cheeks with my thumbs until I felt his body relax and a sigh left his lips. As much as he was a complete asshole, the sound of relief in his sigh made a warmness fill inside of me. I made one last swipe with my thumbs and went to move my hands but his hands went over mine, stopping me.

"Don't stop until you get off of me." His voice was barely a whisper.

Those damn Fallen were still too close by so I relaxed on top of Asher, keeping my thumbs lightly stroking his slightly rough cheek. He needed a shave. I was glad I didn't have to deal with facial hair.

I shifted on top of him and he let out a grunt as my dick rubbed against his erection. His erection? I froze and my hands stilled on his face. Did Asher

Thorne have a boner for me? He despised me, but my own dick didn't care and I let out a frustrated noise as it twitched to life.

"Fuck." Asher gritted out.

I wasn't even entirely sure I liked men sexually. I knew I liked women, but a man? That night Levi had kissed me and I had kissed him back, it hadn't excited me like I thought it would.

"There! Go, go, go!" Shouts and loud feet snapped me out of trying to figure out what I was feeling.

My wings snapped back and I jumped up, holding my hand out to Asher. He glanced at it briefly before getting to his feet on his own and adjusting himself.

The men had taken off down a different hallway so we retraced our steps until we were outside the building. We heard shouting from a distance and moved back around to the front of the building.

"Fuck. They were probably after Toby and Danica."

"Thank you, Captain Obvious." I couldn't keep the snark out of my voice.

He grabbed my arm. "Thanks for that back there. Sometimes I can't stop my brain from freezing up." Then he narrowed his eyes. "And not a word about my dick getting hard."

"I make no promises." I went to walk back towards the lawn in front of the building but he pulled me back and pinned me against the wall, the bumpy surface digging into my elbows.

"Don't fuck with me, angel baby. It won't be pretty." He sounded like he was half beast with his growly voice.

"It felt to me like that's exactly what you wanted. To fuck me." I inwardly cringed at my words.

"The only ass I'll be fucking is Danica's." He shoved himself away from me and took out his phone, cursing at the cracked screen. "They're back at my place. Let's go."

I grabbed him and lifted him with a grunt and took off. He stared at my face until we landed on his roof.

"That's the problem, Danica, you didn't think and you almost got us killed or even worse, captured!"

"I wasn't going to just stand there and watch them take her into that... that... that room!"

Asher and I exchanged glances and rushed to where Danica was jabbing her finger into Tobias's chest. I took Danica's elbow as gently as I could and steered her away before she took a swing at him.

"What happened?"

Danica shook her head and sat on a chair, crossing her arms over her chest. Tobias had his hands on his hips and was shooting daggers at her.

"The plan was to see what they were doing in the operating rooms. They roll them in and out in cages and drain their blood on those grated tables they use in morgues." He shuddered. "And of course, after the angel they drained, they brought in Brooklyn and *she* decided to be a fucking hero." He turned his eyes back to Danica. "Well, I hate to break it to you, but heroes end up dead!"

"I said I was sorry!" Her voice cracked with a sob and she covered her face with her hands.

"Dude, calm down," Asher said, putting his hand on Tobias's shoulder, which he aggressively shoved off.

"It's late. Let's get back to campus. We can meet tomorrow about what we're going to do," I suggested.

"You two go ahead, Toby and I will contact Michael and fill him in."

Danica stood from the chair, keeping her eyes on the ground, and walked to the door leading into Asher's house. I looked back at Asher and I swear he winked at me.

Chapter Sixteen

Danica

I woke up to the sound of my alarm and a grunt in my ear from Olly. Damn, last night had sucked. I hated confrontation and put myself right smack dab in the middle of one with Tobias. Tobias, who was fairly non-confrontational, at least until I started spending more time with him. That was a tough pill to swallow.

I hit the button on my phone and wiggled out of Olly's arms, looking down just as a small smile spread across his lips. He was a beautiful man and if he was a human he would break hearts all over the Los Angeles area.

"Good morning, beautiful," he said, slowly opening his sparkling blue eyes and staring up at me. I could stare into their sparkling depths all day if we didn't have more important things to do like go to class. Oh, and saving Brooklyn and the other angels held captive with her.

He reached for my face and brushed his thumb over my lips. I sighed and stood, adjusting my clothes that had gotten twisted during the night. After driving back last night and crying all over again, I hadn't even bothered changing before falling asleep against Olly's chest.

Olly said nothing as I made my way into the bathroom and shut the door. At least one of us had the ability to stop ourselves from saying or doing something stupid. That's exactly what had happened last night, I was stupid and almost got us caught. Tobias didn't have to yell at me though. I felt bad enough without the raised voice and the looks of irritation.

I looked at myself in the mirror and touched under my eyes. The skin was slightly swollen from not being able to hold anything back anymore. Olly had glued the pieces back together.

I showered quickly and walked back into my room with a towel wrapped around me. Olly was gone, so I dropped my towel and got dressed in my dreaded uniform. I wanted to curl back up in bed and come up with a plan to rescue Brooklyn and the others. That was a pipe dream though. I was not equipped to take on a large group of Fallen. I didn't have immortality on my side.

How was I going to face Cora and Ethan, knowing I had Brooklyn within sight but couldn't rescue her? She had looked really bad when they had rolled her into that room. Not as bad as the angel they had wheeled out before her, but after they drained her she would have looked worse.

I didn't know what I was going to do when I saw Levi. If I had it my way, I would kill him with my bare hands. Except angels were already dead so how to kill one was a mystery to me. Maybe they could be killed the same way as a vampire; heart removal or decapitation. I needed to ask Olly. I would not be asking Tobias. He'd scold me again like I was a child.

Tobias. My chest hurt thinking about last night.

I grabbed my phone and checked my messages. The only one was a group text from Asher telling Olly and I to stay away from Levi and to tell no one what we saw since we didn't know who else was involved.

There was a soft knock on my door as I grabbed my bag. My heart rate increased and I took a deep breath. I wasn't ready to see Tobias, but at least if it happened now, I could rip the Band-Aid off before class and it would be over and done with.

I looked out the peephole and sighed with relief as Olly smiled on the other side. That angel always seemed to be happy. I opened the door and he stepped in the doorway and gave me a hug. I could get lost in his hugs; they felt like a warm blanket fresh out of the dryer.

"How do you already smell like cookies?" I

craned my neck to look up at him. "Don't tell me you bought cookie scented cologne."

"I had cookies for breakfast. Decided to mix it up a little today. Ready to go?"

After trekking across campus together, him holding my hand as we walked, we sat together in class. Today there weren't even any stares or hushed voices discussing what that meant.

I looked at the time on my phone; class should have started five minutes ago, but still no Tobias. A few students had already left, mumbling about him never being late and that they hoped he was okay.

Olly and I were just about to put our stuff away when Dean Whittaker walked in. My favorite person.

"Class is canceled today. Mr. Armstrong is stuck in a meeting. He did want me to tell you that tomorrow there will be a quiz on dream demons and it would behoof you to stay anyway and familiarize yourself with them in your book. You might also use it as an opportunity to ask your classmate about them." She nodded in my direction and then left the room.

I turned to Olly who was running his hand over the cover of the book. "What are you doing?" My question was answered when he moved his hand and the book flopped open to dream demons, my eyes going wide. "Since when did you get all these abilities?"

"I've always had them. Just haven't had a reason

to use them until recently. I don't want to be a show off since the Class IIs and IIIs only have a few things they can do." He looked over at me and gave me a tight smile before his eyes went back to his book. "Sometimes I don't even know that I have an ability until it just happens..."

"What?" I could tell he wanted to say something else.

"Nothing," he said reaching up and touching his hair. "Just learned a little about myself yesterday is all."

"Tell me about it." I opened my book and skimmed the introduction information on dream demons.

Dream demons, also known as night mares, are a highly prevalent psychological demon of hell. The mare is said to be humanoid in form and terrorizes the mind when it enters each REM cycle. It has been rumored, but not confirmed, that these demons walk the Earth unbeknownst to both humans and angels due to its ability to stay hidden.

"Does your dad really have demons here on Earth?" Olly spoke so no one could hear him except me. After yesterday's conversation with him, I'm sure he wasn't the only one that had more questions and probably a plethora of concerns.

"He wouldn't have just made it up. This is probably one of them. He doesn't tell me about *which* demons he has hanging around here."

Olly shuddered and closed his book, putting it in his bag. Most of the other students had already left. I guess they didn't want my expertise, not that I was an expert. I only knew what my father offered.

After hanging out for a while, Olly walked me to PE. Ah, yes, my favorite class. After the snake debacle, Brooklyn's disappearance, and Levi being in the class, I considered going to the library and studying. Most instructors would notice I was missing, since they always seemed to keep an eye on me, so I sucked it up and changed.

Walking into the gym, I scanned and easily found Coach Ferguson talking with Levi. I squared my shoulders and walked towards them. Coach Ferguson had an extreme dislike for me, and Levi, well, I would have said he was working for the devil, but that wasn't true.

"Deville. Wright has offered to work with you today." Before I could protest, he turned and walked away. I clenched my hands, digging my nails into my palms to keep from popping off some comment.

I could do this. I could get through an hour with a monster. Or not. I started making my way back towards the locker room but he grabbed my arm and steered me towards the training room. I yanked my arm away and rubbed where he grabbed. It hadn't exactly been a loving touch.

"Don't touch me again," I warned as we entered the room.

I suddenly felt very vulnerable being somewhat alone with him. We could still see the rest of the class, but there were also several spots in the room where the rest of the gym was out of sight. I'd avoid those like the plague.

"Or what, Dee? You'll sic your angel boyfriends on me?" he taunted, walking to a cabinet and pulling out two focus mitts and slipping them onto his hands. "Now let's see what you got before I kick your ass."

I scoffed and crossed my arms. "Don't call me Dee, and if you think I'm going to fight with you then-" In a quick jab, he knocked me over the side of the head with his mitt. "You fucking asshole."

I could have just turned around and left the room, but the opportunity was too great to let it slip through my fingers. I had half expected him not to show his face on campus again, yet here he was, acting as if he wasn't a traitor.

"My beef isn't with you, *Dee.*" He hit me again, this time hard enough to make me stumble back.

I positioned my body to strike back and he held up the mitts with a satisfied smirk on his face. I took several punches and dodged several of his swipes.

"Who is your beef with then?" *Punch, punch, duck.*

"Angels." He kicked out with his foot and tripped me. I grunted as my ass hit the mat. "Get up."

"You're an angel. Why?" *Punch, punch, duck, jump back.*

We ran through several more combinations before he answered. "Do you know how I died?"

I stopped mid-punch and his mitt slammed into my face. It stung and I rubbed my nose. "How?"

"I was texting and speeding." He swept out and knocked me down again. "Two lane road."

I stood up again and backed up as he took another swipe at me. He had a determined glint in his eyes, like he wanted to take out all of his anger on me.

"How do you know that? I thought they just told you in general how you died, like a car crash." I backed up, avoiding his increasingly aggressive kicks and jabs. I took a deep breath as he stopped in front of me.

"I'm not an idiot. I used Google." I flinched as he punched the wall at the side of my head. That would have hurt.

"And what did Google tell you?" I whispered.

"I was going over a hundred. What do you think it told me?" he asked through clenched teeth. He punched the wall on the other side of my head, with a lot less force, but now I was trapped between his arms.

I shut my eyes for a brief moment before opening them and searching his tormented green eyes. "Did you crash into another car?"

Nod.

"Were there people inside?"

Nod.

"Did they survive?"

Shake.

The only sounds in the room were his deep breathing, my heartbeat, and Mr. Miller's booming voice shouting directions.

"I deserve to be in hell." He backed away from me and threw the mitts off to the side. "And now I'll get what I deserve. And with what I've done, they won't even bother making me a Fallen. They will send me straight to hell like they should have done in the first place."

My heart was thudding wildly in my chest. I felt a twinge of sympathy, but also a whole lot of anger that he would betray angels just to give himself a punishment. "How did you even get involved with them?"

"A few months ago, they took me when I was at the arcade. They offer all the angels they take the opportunity to work with them or be drained daily." He shrugged, like it was no big deal. "It was a win-win. They'd get their insider and eventually I'd get a one-way ticket to hell."

"Do you know what they're planning on doing with all the blood?" As soon as the words left my mouth, he laughed. It wasn't a normal laugh, but the laugh of a crazy person; a broken person. Maybe at some point he had been sane, but now he had gotten himself in too deep, let his past eat away at his future.

"Danica." Tobias's voice came from the doorway and I turned to see him, the dean, and Michael standing there. He stared at me for a moment, not showing an ounce of emotion and then turned and walked towards Levi. "Levi, you need to come with us."

"Nice talk, Dee. Tell Oliver I'm sorry for leading him on," he said, following Tobias with his head hanging.

I stood in the doorway and watched them exit out of the gym.

~

BY THE TIME school was done, I was mentally exhausted. It was hard keeping it together on a normal day, but trying to focus and have everything else in my life going on? Impossible.

A group text came shortly after dinner from Tobias. *Meet us at Asher's. Oliver, fly with her.*

Butterflies filled my stomach at the thought of having to face Tobias. He had consumed my thoughts all day. Maybe he'd be over it by now and we could just move on. I had fucked up and he had acted like a dickwad about it.

We landed on the roof to find Asher and Tobias roasting marshmallows over the fire pit like they were boy scouts on a camping trip. I smiled to myself. They had the whole bromance vibe going on and I hoped they would start including Olly more. He needed it.

I flopped down in one of the empty chairs next to Tobias and stared into the fire. It was the perfect night for sitting around a fire outside. Not too cold, but just cold enough to need something other than a jacket.

"Angel baby, have you ever had a s'more?" Asher asked, turning the metal rod he had speared through a marshmallow in the flames. He pulled the marshmallow out and blew out the flame, the white covered in bumpy brown and black.

"Can't say I have," he responded, his eyes lighting up as he watched Asher with curiosity.

"Well, first you take the graham, stick the chocolate on the graham." Asher already had the marshmallow cooked so he smooshed it all together and handed to Olly. "Tada, a s'more."

We watched as Olly took a bite and a grin lit up his face. It would be nice to feel that kind of wonder again, like every moment of the day was a new gift being unwrapped. I bet he'd never been to Disneyland and my list of fun places to go and things to do was slowly growing inside my head. We needed an Olly bucket list.

"Drinks?" Asher asked, standing and wiping his hands on his jeans, leaving graham cracker crumbs behind.

"I'll take a water," I said, staring back into the fire, getting lost in the mesmerizing flicker of colors.

Tobias's eyes darted over to me with a questioning look. It seemed like every time I was drinking something, it was Diet Dr. Pepper. It was a problem, but everyone seemed to have their vice.

"I was doing some research online about natural remedies to my inattentive impulsivity issue. Drinking a six pack of diet soda a day is probably not helping any." I propped my chin up on my fist and looked at Tobias. "Right?"

"I'll join you to get the drinks," Olly said, standing and following Asher inside. I just hoped they didn't kill each other in there without supervision.

Tobias took a drink of his beer before leaning forward to assemble a s'more and offering it to me without a word. I shook my head.

"So... the silent treatment? Never took you for the silent treatment type. Seems below you." I grabbed a marshmallow and stabbed it with the metal roasting fork.

"I think I said enough last night." Tobias bit into his s'more, getting some marshmallow on his beard. I wanted to reach over and wipe it off but refrained. The last thing I wanted was for him to pull away from my touch.

I nodded and slowly turned the marshmallow just out of reach of the flames. I liked my marshmallows golden brown, not burned to a crisp.

Despite my less-than-traditional upbringing, my dad did still teach me a thing or two. Like how to not burn a marshmallow.

"You yelled at me like I was your child instead of your girlfriend."

I brought the marshmallow to my lips and blew on it, the sweetness filling my nose and making my mouth water. I could feel him watching me as I bit into it and then had to use my fingers to break the sticky strings holding onto the other half. I licked my fingers and sighed.

"I know you were pissed and scared, and I respect that was how you felt, but yelling at me? I couldn't just stand there and watch them hurt my friend, or anyone for that matter. I know it was stupid, and reckless, and horribly impulsive. I already feel like enough of a fuck up. I don't need you to remind me of it by yelling at me or giving me the silent treatment." I popped the other half of the marshmallow in my mouth.

"You aren't a fuck up." He moved his chair closer to me, the sound of the metal legs scraping on the roof. He grabbed my wrist and brought my sticky fingers to his lips. "I just really like you and you could have been hurt or killed."

I shut my eyes as he put my fingers in his mouth and swirled his tongue around them. He pulled them out with a pop and yanked my arm towards him, pulling me onto his lap. I laced my fingers behind his neck and put my forehead against his.

"If you ever yell at me again, I *will* spank you." He made a noise in his throat and slid his hand under my shirt to rest on my side.

"The only one that will be doing any spanking is me." I shivered as his cold hand moved up my stomach and traced the band of my bra. "What color is it?"

"Black." He made a satisfied noise in his throat at my answer and kissed my neck.

We heard the door to the roof open and Olly and Asher sat back down. I looked over at them and sighed as Tobias continued to pepper my neck with kisses. I pulled away, but stayed in his lap. I wasn't sure what the etiquette was for PDA in front of your other boyfriends.

"So, what are our next steps with the Fallen?"

"For you two?" Asher pointed at me and Olly with his beer. "Nothing. We went with a few of the archangels and Michael's soldiers last night back to St. Luke and they had already moved their entire operation. They must have an older angel working with them because no one could get a read on them."

I went to move off Tobias's lap, but he held me in place, his fingers digging into my waist.

"They've been recruiting on the streets. Now that Levi isn't going to be interfering and none of them saw Asher, he's going to go undercover and find out where they are. We don't know how long it's going to take for him to infiltrate. They're probably going to be very cautious now."

"What about your business?" What I really wanted to say was, 'what about me.?' It was a selfish thing to think, but the idea of him joining them made me sick to my stomach.

"I have foremen who will run things while I'm gone. I won't be able to come back here until this is all over. I won't risk them ruining this part of my life." Asher swirled the beer that was left in his bottle and drank it down. "Let's go inside. I'm getting cold."

I should have known when we all sat on the couch that things were going to take an interesting turn. Especially when Asher turned off the lights, the only light coming from a lamp by the bed and the television.

It started with Asher's hand rubbing my leg in slow circles. He had a slight smirk on his face, like he knew exactly what he was doing. I felt the tips of my ears burn slightly at the thought of him touching me in front of the others. My legs parted slightly and I saw Tobias glance over at the move-ment and watch Asher as he trailed his hand up and down my inner thigh along the seam of my jeans. I could already feel the wetness building between my legs.

He raised his eyebrows at Asher and then put his hand on my other thigh, massaging it with firm squeezes. I just about let out a moan at the thought of both of them touching my naked body. Would they even want to do something like that? I was down for anything, but we hadn't exactly discussed how it was going to work when we were all together and they all wanted me.

"Boys, behave," I whispered, looking over at Olly. Now I really wished I hadn't been taking things slow with him because I was pretty sure by the way the other two were touching me that they were in the mood and didn't care if they had to share.

It's not like we could go into another room. I mean there was the bathroom, but I didn't want my first threesome to be in a bathroom.

Olly was so engrossed in watching the Marvel action flick he picked, he wasn't even paying us any attention. At least not yet.

Asher turned his body towards me and kissed my neck, trailing his hand to cup me between the legs. I bit my lip and tried to focus on the movie. Tobias took my hand and kissed my wrist before slowly moving up my arm with his lips. I squirmed slightly, feeling the tickling between my legs increase, the need to be touched already reaching a point of discomfort.

"What are you doing?" I sighed and slid on the couch so I could rest my neck on the back cushion.

"Are you complaining?" Asher kissed under my ear before moving his hand to unbutton my jeans.

My breath got louder and I sank into the couch as Tobias's hand moved up my shirt and Asher slipped his hand into my pants, cupping my wet panties.

"How long do you think it will take for angel baby over there to notice anything is going on?" Asher said once Tobias had moved his lips to the other side of my neck.

"I think the bigger question is what is he going to do when he does look over here," Tobias said, glancing in his direction.

"Pull your pants down a little. They're too tight," Asher mumbled against my neck, his fingers tracing around my belly button.

A hand slipped back under my shirt and pushed my bra up over my breasts, giving easy access to my nipples. I lifted my ass and slid my pants and panties down. Asher's hand found my clit and leisurely moved his fingers across it. I stifled my moan and glanced over at Olly.

I half expected him not to notice, but his eyes met mine. He put a finger to his lips to tell me to be quiet. The gesture had me closing my eyes and putting my head back on the couch.

"Do you want him to see?" Tobias kissed down my jaw. "We can stop."

"Don't stop," I moaned, finally giving in to the sounds my body wanted to make.

Tobias moved off the couch and knelt in front of me, taking off my pants the rest of the way and spreading my legs. Asher took care of my shirt and bra. Olly took in an audible gulp of air and my eyes went back to him. His eyes were locked on my exposed pussy as Tobias kneaded my inner thighs and then pulled me to the edge of the couch and buried his face between my legs.

"Fuck..." My hips bucked as his tongue dived into me, his thumb circling my clit. His mouth devoured me like I was his last supper.

Asher moved his lips to mine and pulled my lip between his teeth as I moved my hand to his pants and unbuttoned them. Out of the corner of my eye I watched Olly unbutton his own pants and pull out his cock. The thought of all three of them at once sent the first wave of pleasure crashing through my body, my legs trying to squeeze shut and my body shaking.

Asher stood and took off his pants, grabbing the base of his dick and pumping it a few times. "How do we want to do this?"

I couldn't help it, I giggled. Maybe it was all the endorphins from my orgasm or the sheer fact we were about to have a very awkward conversation.

"Smooth man, real smooth." Tobias rolled his eyes and leisurely moved his thumb over my clit, sending lightning bolt jolts up my spine. He looked over at Olly who sat quietly stroking himself. "Are you going to join in?"

"I just want to watch tonight. If that's okay with Danica." He looked at me with an almost embarrassed look on his face. I gave him a nod of approval.

I pulled myself up so I was sitting and clamped my legs shut, my clit needing a brief break from the assault Tobias had rained down upon it. I looked up at the men in front of me, in various states of undress.

I grabbed Asher's hand and tugged him down so he was on top of me, my legs wrapping around his waist. He moaned against my lips as he grinded into me, his dick moving across my folds. He pulled back and put my calves over his shoulders before slowly sinking into me with a groan.

"Fuck, this will never get old," he said, kissing one of my calves and moving slowly, almost obnoxiously slow, like he was savoring every thrust. Tobias watched us, dick in hand, like he was trying to figure out what his next move was.

"Come here. I want you in my mouth." I licked my lips and waited for him to take the two steps to the couch. I couldn't exactly reach him from my spot. "Kneel behind my head, then you can watch."

Asher moved one of my legs to drape on the back of the couch, giving an unobstructed view to both me and Tobias. Tobias climbed on the couch on his knees, his dick hanging in front of my lips. I took him in my mouth, one of my hands wrapping firmly around the base.

The room filled with moans as Asher's pace increased and my mouth sucked and licked Tobias. I heard a sharp inhale of breath from the other end of the couch and then a shaky exhale. I had almost forgotten that Olly was watching and the thought of him coming all over his hand as he got off on seeing the three of us was almost too much.

"Harder," I mumbled around Tobias's cock. He groaned and leaned forward on one hand, the other going to my clit. His hips were slowly thrusting his cock deeper in my throat, stifling my moans.

"I'm going to fucking come if you do that," Asher growled as his thrusts became harder and more erratic. I knew exactly what he was talking about when I felt Tobias's mouth close around my clit and suck it between his teeth.

My entire body seemed to combust as Asher thrust into me hard and spilled himself in my clenching pussy. I cried out around Tobias's cock, moving one of my hands to his balls and massaging them. He came with a curse, spilling into my mouth.

I swallowed and pulled him out of my mouth, my heart beating wildly, my breaths short and deep. My ears were ringing and my toes felt like they had just woken up from falling asleep.

Tobias plopped back next to my head and smoothed his fingers across my forehead. "I'm glad I wasn't a stubborn asshole about this whole concept."

Asher pulled out of me, the emptiness without him making me shiver. He pulled a blanket from the back of the couch and threw it over me. "That was fucking mind-blowing." He pulled my legs into his lap and ran his hands over my blanketed calves. We sat in comfortable silence for a few minutes, catching our breaths.

"How is it going to work with three of us?" Olly was buttoning up his pants and didn't look up. If blushing had a sound, it would have been the sound of his voice.

"We'll make it work, angel baby. When you're ready to join, we'll take care of you," Asher said, surprising the shit out of me. I looked at Asher who was looking at Olly with a small smile turning up the corners of his lips.

"So about that name... angel baby. It's not very creative. Last night I thought it would be cool if we had walkie talkies or those secret service ear pieces. Then we could have those nicknames people say on them. Danica's could be something with sexy in it. Tobias could be Dirty Teach or something. Asher, you could be Whiskey Dick. What do you guys think of Golden Cherub for me?"

The perfect way to end the night was wiping tears off my face from laughing so hard.

Chapter Seventeen

Asher

*T*he name Danica means 'the morning star' which I discovered when I Googled her after we first met. I might not have known her for very long, but she was the first thing I thought about in the morning. She was *my* morning star. Which made it that much harder that I couldn't see her, talk to her, or even fucking text her.

I groaned as I rolled over on the crappy mattress in a crappy motel just on the outskirts of downtown Los Angeles. Five years ago I wouldn't have given a shit about a lumpy mattress with questionable stains on the bedspread, but now I cared. I could never go back to that life; the life of a lost Fallen.

With my third day undercover behind me, it seemed this mission was futile. I never thought I'd be on another mission, but here I was, following

Michael's orders yet again. It better be fucking worth it.

I sat up and cradled my head in my hands, rubbing my temples. The last few weeks had reopened wounds I had thought were mostly behind me. I had a routine with familiar places, people, sounds, smells. Now the mild comfort it had given me had vanished and was replaced by a tightness in my gut that only disappeared when Danica was around. Or when Oliver touched me.

I TOSSED and turned on the couch, willing myself to sleep. I hadn't wanted to try to infiltrate the Fallen. There were too many unknown variables, but Michael had convinced me that if I helped then he would personally escort me to another review board hearing.

On the eve of uncertainty, I found myself back in the trenches, gunfire whizzing past my ears, blood soaking my clothing. I let out a frustrated grunt and made my way to the bathroom. I glanced in the direction of the bed where three forms were sleeping peacefully. Lucky bastards.

I shut the door and looked at myself in the mirror. I looked like shit and gripped the edge of the counter in frustration. Why couldn't it all just fucking stop?

The bathroom door slid open and my head snapped in that direction, my heartrate increasing. Another unknown variable taunting me. Oliver slid in, sliding the door shut behind him.

"Are you okay?" He looked and sounded half asleep, his eyes squinting at the bright light in the bathroom.

"Not your problem," I said between clenched teeth. I just wanted to be alone and I most certainly didn't want to be bothered by Oliver, who half the time used my last slivers of patience.

He walked farther into the large bathroom and leaned his hip against the vanity. I felt his eyes on me and looked at him again.

"Do you need to take a piss or what?" I let go of the counter and crossed my arms over my bare chest, feeling exposed, which was interesting considering he had just watched Toby and I have sex with Danica.

"I heard you on the couch and was worried. You could come sleep with us in the bed." He moved away from the vanity and blocked my path out of the bathroom.

I stared at him. Man, he had some cojones coming into the bathroom like this. I moved forward to step around him and he grabbed my arm. My knees nearly gave out as a wave of calmness washed over me.

"I'll sleep right next to you. You don't have to sleep alone anymore," he said softly.

I felt my eyes burning with tears and kept my eyes glued to his hand on my forearm. I cleared my throat. "Can't risk it. I'd never forgive myself if I did something in my sleep."

"Then let me sleep with you on the couch." His hand squeezed my arm and he started moving towards the door, not letting go.

I followed him, unable to resist whatever comfort he was

giving me. It was more intense than it had been back at the hospital when he had fallen on top of me.

He laid down on the couch on his side and looked up at me. I glanced at the bottle of whiskey sitting open on the coffee table and then back at him. He shook his head and patted the couch. Fuck.

I sat down and felt his hand touch the middle of my back. I took a deep breath and laid down, his chest against my back, his arms wrapping around me.

THE MEMORY of the best night's sleep I had ever had plagued me as I grabbed my wrinkled clothes off the chair and put them on. Oliver was now on my mind almost as frequently as Danica and I didn't know if I liked it or not.

For the past three nights I had wandered the streets and nothing came of it. I was sleep deprived and I smelled like something the cat dragged in. I don't know what Michael really expected, for them to just come up to me and recruit me?

It was just before sunrise and traffic was virtually nonexistent in this area. I passed a few shops and bars as I made my way away from the motel and turned down an alley. I had been frequenting this alley since it had large painted angel wings on the brick. That had to mean something, right?

I leaned against the wall, my back right in the center of those damn wings, and waited. There was no way that someone would paint these down a narrow alley unless they meant something, at least that was what I kept telling myself.

I waited for an hour and then pushed off the wall, shuffling the rest of the way down the alley. It was fucking depressing here. Years ago I was living this way, moving around aimlessly, sleeping in doorways, sleeping on sidewalks.

I exited the alley and made my way past makeshift tents made of ripped blue tarps, sleeping figures in sleeping bags, countless shopping carts. Where were the guardian angels when these people needed them? Clearly their own damn people didn't care enough to have a shred of humanity. And here I was being a hypocrite because I didn't help them myself.

I took a seat on the curb and ran my hands through my tangled and greasy hair. I had only encountered a few Fallen the past few nights, but they were all solo and high or drunk out of their minds. I might have been out here for weeks before I even encountered the Fallen I was after.

I'm not one that really believes that things happen because you're thinking about them, but sure as shit, not a minute after wallowing in the idea of spending more time out here, a gray van turned down the street and slowly made its way in my direction. I could sense two of them in the van. They were going slow because they could sense me too.

The van pulled in just past where I was and

then stopped. I kept my eyes fixed on the ground until a pair of black combat boots came into my line of sight.

"Hey, man. You look like you could use a warm meal and a shower. Interested?"

I looked up and squinted at the Fallen in front of me. He needed to work on his delivery because that sounded like a fucking proposition. Literally.

"What's the price? I'm not into dicks."

The guy held his hands up in front of himself in defense. "Woah, man. Not like that. Just trying to help out a brother who's down on his luck."

"I'm not your brother," I said, standing and nodding my chin towards the van. "You and your buddy murdering homeless Fallen?"

He laughed and put out his hand. I could see why this guy was the one to approach me; he was charming in a serial killer type of way. "Name's Paul. If you'll come to breakfast, I might have a job opportunity for you."

I eyed his hand warily. I had to make this shit believable because if I was too eager then they might question my sanity. The goal was to get in and get close fast.

"I don't know, man. My mom told me to never get into a van with a stranger." I grabbed his hand and shook it. "But I guess since my mom is dead and I am too, what else do I have to lose?"

"That's the spirit." He smacked me on the arm

and then made his way to the van, opening the back door. "What's your name?"

"Tom," I lied. Although it wasn't a complete lie since my middle name was Thomas. There was no fucking way I was giving those idiots my real name.

I climbed in the back of the van and he shut the door behind me. It was clean and smelled faintly of bleach. Always a good sign when getting into a creepy ass van with complete strangers.

The van took off and I reached down and pressed the button on the inside tongue of my boot. It was a one-way communication and tracking device that would record my location and anything that was said.

"Where are we going? I'm claustrophobic as fuck, man!" I shouted, hoping they'd hear me.

I didn't get a reply so I just sat back and tried to calm myself down. Wherever they were taking me, they didn't want me to know.

I WAS IN. After some convincing on their part, I agreed to join them. The only problem was that to actually beat them, I was going to have to do some morally questionable things, like help capture angels.

Coming into this whole thing, Michael had warned me that they would probably have me prove myself before I even learned where they were holed up. I just hadn't expected it to be so quickly, but I guess they were desperate.

Paul fed me, made me shower, convinced me to be a part of his team, and twelve hours later I was riding with him and another Fallen named Jimmy. They were desperate for more angels, saying their supply in Pasadena dried up.

"What do you do, just drive around all night?" I was in the passenger seat with Jimmy, sitting in the middle of the bench seat. "Seems a little unorganized."

"We were organized in Pasadena, were doing well capturing angels for a while but then three of our teams got taken out."

I grunted a response and looked out the window at the passing buildings. "Have you tried hospitals?"

"Too risky. We know they're there a lot, but we can never sense them."

"What about a trap where we don't necessarily need to sense them?" I was actually surprised they flew by the seats of their pants most of the time. From my understanding they had been abducting angels for over two months and had two dozen somewhere.

"What kind of trap? We try not to draw human attention." I could hear the concern in Jimmy's voice.

"What's the first rule of Fight Club?" I crossed my arms over my chest and turned slightly towards them.

"You do not talk about Fight Club. What's your point? You got a hard-on for Pitt?" Jimmy rolled his eyes and looked moderately annoyed.

"I did a rotation during my guardian days as a security guard. The security guards are always guardians. No special medical skills needed, and no one questions why they wander the floor and go in rooms. There's typically only one guardian per department. I'll just go in there and start screaming about angels. Lure one out." I was surprised at how calm my voice sounded with the lies spewing out of it.

"And if the security isn't a guardian?" Paul was tapping one of his hands on the steering wheel. I could tell the idea excited him.

I shrugged. "We'll know as soon as we spray him with that shit you have and we can either take him anyway and dump him or just let him go. If this works we can hit several hospitals."

"Where should we start?" Paul asked, pulling over and getting out his phone. He was the only one of us that had one. I didn't bother bringing mine since I knew they would have taken it.

"Nearest hospital." It didn't matter where we went, the guardians would be ready and make a show of it.

Ten minutes later, Jimmy sat in the driver's seat and I made my way to the emergency room doors after letting Paul take several swings at me. With blood pouring out of my nose, I walked in the sliding door and went right up to the reception desk.

"I need to see an angel." The man and woman that were sitting at the desk had already started to rise as I had approached the desk.

"Sir, we'll have a nurse to get the bleeding to stop and it will be a couple of hours to see a doctor."

I laughed at the woman's words and slammed my fists down on the desk, leaving blood smeared on the counter.

"I said I want to see a fucking angel. So either go find one or I will-"

"I got this," the security guard said from behind me.

I spun around and took a swing at him, but he stopped my fist with his hand and wrenched my arm behind my back, a little too hard for my liking. He shoved me forward and we stepped out of the sliding doors.

Everything happened in a blur then. I twisted away from him, Paul sprayed him with demon blood serum, and then I snapped his neck. Completely not part of the plan, but shit, my shoulder still stung from him twisting it.

Paul stared at me and shook his head as Jimmy pulled up beside us. We secured the angel's arms and legs and tossed him in the back.

We hit three more hospitals, resulting in a total of four angels with snapped necks. They were easier to deal with being incapacitated completely, but would heal in a day or two. Paul dropped Jimmy off and we were on the I-110 South headed towards the Port of Los Angeles, straight to the heart of the beast.

Chapter Eighteen

Danica

*O*ver two weeks had passed since Asher went undercover with the Fallen. Whatever was happening, we weren't privy to it, not even Tobias. It was completely understandable since we had gone rogue in our attempts to find out what the Fallen were doing. Classes continued, weird stares and hushed comments followed me, and a small feeling of normalcy crept back into my life.

"I want to drive your car," Olly announced after a movie finished. I should have known something like this would happen after watching *The Fast and the Furious*.

Olly and I had fallen into a comfortable pattern of movie watching before dinner and studying. Sometimes we would even watch the entire movie instead of making out the whole time.

"Excuse me? You want to drive *my* car?" I laughed at the absurdity. "Do you even know how to drive?"

"It can't be that hard, can it?"

Laughter bubbled out of me at the vision of him trying to drive a car. I mulled over his words and shrugged my shoulders. Everyone has to start somewhere.

"We aren't supposed to leave campus."

He made a dismissive sound. "It's the middle of the day and I'm starting to feel claustrophobic being stuck here, kind of like I used to feel when I was in heaven. If we don't go then I'm bound to do something stupid." He poked my ribs and stood up, offering me his hand. "Maybe when we're done we can park somewhere and make out."

I grinned up at him and let him pull me to my feet. I could totally get on board with a make out session in the car, especially with him. We hadn't slept together yet, but we had certainly been having fun building up to it.

I drove to a high school parking lot and let him slide behind the wheel of my baby. I explained the basics and made sure he understood what each pedal did before I let him put it into drive. This was either going to go surprisingly well or I would finally understand how parents feel when teaching their kids to drive.

He caught on quickly and after a solid thirty minutes of driving at a snail's pace around the parking lot we switched back. No lives were lost in the parking lot during our lesson, although I felt like I might have a bit of whiplash from all the stopping and starting we did in the beginning. Next time he'd probably be ready to drive around a housing tract with extra wide streets. Maybe. If it wasn't trash day.

I slid back behind the wheel and smiled over at Olly before leaning over and giving him a kiss. He grinned ear to ear and I matched his glee. The closer I got to him, the more I realized how hard his short life had been. Small experiences that so many other angels had as human or angel just weren't in his schema of the world.

We pulled out onto the road and then the highway, heading back towards campus. The sun was setting, making the sky glow a beautiful blend of coral, pink, and purple. Olly put his hand on my thigh as I drove, a comfortable silence falling between us, with the radio playing in the background.

Angeles Crest Highway finally wound its way into the rocky hills and the Angeles National Forest sign greeted us as we started winding our way along the two-lane highway. On the driver's side was the opposite lane and the rock face, and on the passenger side were the slopes of hills and mountains and splattering of guard rails when needed. I enjoyed this drive, feeling like I was on a rollercoaster. Even if I had wings, I wouldn't give up the feel of asphalt against my tires and the relaxing lull of controlling a beautiful piece of machinery.

"I don't think I'll be ready to drive like this for a while," Olly said with a laugh.

"You learned quickly today. I half expected to yell at you or slam my foot on the invisible brake pedal on the passenger side. I was lucky I had already driven plenty of go karts before actually driving a car."

"Is that something we can do too? Drive go karts?"

"We can do anything you want. I'm sure Asher and Tobias would like to tag along too."

We passed a turnout that had a viewpoint looking out over the hills with the city in the distance. Olly moved his hand off my leg and turned in his seat to look out the passenger window as we passed and then twisted towards me to look out the back window.

"A gray van and a truck just pulled out after us." I clenched the steering wheel at his words and looked in the rearview mirror. The truck was about four car lengths behind. Olly had his eyes shut. "There are three Fallen in the van and three in the truck."

"Call Tobias." Olly had his phone out and to his ear before I finished speaking.

We were approaching another viewpoint, and just as we were at the entrance, the truck gunned its engine, moved into the other lane, and sent me spinning into the lot for the viewpoint. I could hear Tobias yelling on the other end of the phone as it flew out of Olly's hand on impact and landed somewhere on the floor.

Everything was a blur as the car came to a screeching halt. I must have slammed on the brakes at some point because the smell of burned rubber filled my nose and made me gag. We had no time before they were on us. The van, the truck, another van that had been waiting.

The doors ripped open and both of us were pulled from the seats and thrown to the ground. I caught a brief flash of white as Olly's wings extended but saw him on the ground with a net over him. Our eyes met, the fear in his matching my own.

I managed to stagger to my feet. Most of the men were surrounding Olly now, his fight fierce, but no match for the net that was more than likely doused in demon blood. One of the Fallen grabbed Olly's head and gave it a sharp twist, snapping it.

Rough hands picked me up and slammed me back into the cement and a steel-toe boot kicked me in the ribs. Pain filled my body and I coughed as my chest got tight. I felt like a thousand pounds were sitting on my chest. I could taste blood in my mouth and a cry lodged in my throat as my hands were jerked behind me and metal clicked around my wrists.

"Get them in the vans," a rough voice

commanded as I was yanked to my feet by my hair, a wet cry leaving my throat.

My ears rang with a high-pitched fuzziness as I was dragged to one of the vans. My vision sparked with pops of color before going black. I was jolted awake as my body was slammed onto the cold metal of the van before I was knocked out again.

HANDS WERE UNDER MY ARMPITS. The hands set me on something cold and hard. I couldn't see or even really hear, but I could feel. Drops of something warm hit my face. There were two blurry blobs off to the side of me. The voices were muffled for a while and then I heard an agonizing cry before the pain took me back to darkness.

PAIN. So much pain. *Just let me die already*. Every bone in my body had to be broken. It felt like my eyeballs were ripped to shreds. Was my skin on fire? A scream ripped out of my throat causing me to cough and splutter. Everything went numb and I felt my body floating upwards. *Finally*.

AWARENESS RETURNED to me before my body was fully awake. Cold concrete. The smell of blood. *Fuck.* I was in hell. I think. I never asked my dad what happened when you got sent to hell. Where was he?

Drip. Drip. Drip. The sound echoed in my skull and I jerked awake, my eyes going to a sink in the corner. On the other side of thick medal bars. What in the hell?

I moved my eyes around the room, everything clear in the dim light filtering down from a single lightbulb at the top of the staircase. Nothing good ever came from a basement with a single light bulb.

I was in a cage against a far wall, all four sides being reinforced with two-inch diameter steel rods. Chains were bolted to the floor. Four. One for each limb. Luckily, they weren't attached to me.

I ran my hands over my body; it was perfectly intact but caked with blood and dirt, among other things. This was some next level shit I was in. I reached through the bars and grabbed a water bottle that sat just within my reach. I ripped open the bottle, chugging the entire contents in one gulp. My throat was so raw it felt like I had swallowed shards of glass, or maybe that had been from my screams.

The basement was the size of a small apartment with a staircase leading up to a door, and another door on the far side of the room. There was also a table with slats in it and a basin off the side of it. It was an autopsy table.

Bile rose in my throat and I swallowed it down as I racked my brain for what had happened. The Fallen had captured us. They snapped Olly's neck. Then there was lots and lots of pain. The thought of the pain made me wretch, sending the water I had just gulped out onto the floor. My stomach felt like it was in a million knots, twisting tighter by the minute.

The click of a lock at the top of the stairs ripped me from my agony and I felt panic rising in my chest. I quickly laid down and curled in a ball facing the wall. Maybe they would leave me alone if they thought I was still passed out.

Three sets of footsteps made their way down the stairs. Oh God, where was Olly?

One set of feet sounded heavy, as if the person didn't really give a shit, another was a pair of heels, and the last was firm and sure.

I tried to control my breathing as they approached. They stopped what sounded like a few feet from the bars. Several long minutes passed, and I wondered why they were so quiet.

"How long has she been out? He healed her. She should be awake by now." A woman spoke, her voice sending a slight shiver through my body.

"Just over twenty-four hours. Do you want us to try to wake her?" a gruff voice asked, stepping closer as he spoke.

"Wait until I'm gone. What is the status of our supply?"

"We are at eighty percent of what is needed. The archangel has been an added benefit, but if we drain *him* too much he can't heal the rest."

The woman made a sound of annoyance in her throat and then her heels moved back towards the stairs. "Make sure she's fed and cleaned."

Her heel taps faded as she climbed the stairs and exited the door. I trembled slightly, feeling their eyes boring into my back. A set of keys jingled and the sound of the metal lock clicking made me whimper.

"Do you need help?" The gruff voice spoke again from the same spot he had been in. "I don't think I can stomach this shit, man. She's not even a fucking angel. You clean her up. I'll lock the door just in case and go get some food for her."

"You do that." Asher's voice nearly caused me to jump up and fling myself at him, but I bit down on my knuckle instead, holding back the sob that was threatening to spill out.

He was here.

He was going to save me. Save Olly.

The heavy feet retreated up the stairs and the lock slid into place after the door was closed. Asher let out a shaky breath and opened my prison, kneeling next to me.

"Hun... I'm so fucking sorry." He pulled me into his arms, my body shaking with sobs and fear. "I need to hurry and get you cleaned up before he comes back."

He scooped me in his arms, not caring how completely nasty I was, and walked past the autopsy table and to the door on the other side. Inside was a bathroom, a gross looking bathroom, but it had a shower, toilet, and sink.

He set me down on the toilet lid and went back into the room. I heard him opening a cabinet and then he came back with a towel, washcloth, and what looked like scrubs. He turned on the shower and pulled me up.

"Where are we?" My words left my lips, my teeth chattering. I wasn't cold, but my body was reacting to the bone deep fear coursing through my body.

I had thought fear was sitting outside the principal's office waiting for my dad. Watching horror movies with the lights off at night. Having to talk to the police about the joint in my locker. I was wrong about what fear felt like.

"Port of Los Angeles. They plan on taking a ship with the angel blood out into the Pacific and creating another gate to hell." I let him take off my clothes as he talked. "This has been in the works for a long time, Danica. Years. That woman and some fucker named Adamson are the masterminds behind it all."

My hands gripped Asher's forearms. "John Adamson?" My heart had already been beating fast, now it was reaching its peak. Could a heart explode? I was pretty sure mine was about to.

"You know him? Or them? There's two of them, although the kid was only here once." I loosened my grip and he moved me into the warm water of the shower. He grabbed a washcloth and began cleaning me. I let him because my mind couldn't even handle what was happening.

"I punched that fucker in the nose because he was trying to get me to join his 'church' to be a dealer."

Asher silently cleaned my body and hair without speaking. He was processing that new information. Hell, I was processing that information. He shut off the water and started to dry me off.

"So this goes even deeper than we thought. Your dad is going to lose his shit even more than he already is. It took four angels to restrain him and keep him from coming to get you. I think that's what they want."

"John Adamson Senior was my doctor. He delivered me. He's known this whole time."

I stepped into the scrub bottoms Asher held open for me, balancing myself by putting my hands on his shoulders. "Who's the woman?"

Asher pulled the scrub top over my head and ran his hands over my arms.

"She says she has no name like we're in *Game of Thrones* or some shit. She wears a scarf around her head and sunglasses even inside so I don't even really know what she looks like. Listen, we don't have much time before Paul gets back."

He pulled me to him and hugged me, raking his fingers over my tangled wet hair. He lowered his voice to a whisper. "After sunset tonight all hell is going to break loose on this place. I'm going to pretend to lock the cell and then unlock the door upstairs later. You can't try to escape until you hear all the noise. Okay?" He pulled back and looked in my face. "I will be freeing the others and you need to run. Take a right at the top of the stairs and just run. No matter what you hear or see. Do you understand?"

I nodded.

"No. I need to hear that you understand." Tears were in his eyes. "What's out there... promise me you will turn right and run."

"I promise I'll turn right and run, no matter what."

He let out a sigh of relief and scooped me back into his arms to carry me back to my cage. Just as he was shutting the door, the lock turned at the top of the stairs.

"I love you, Danica."

I wish I could have said it back to him before Paul came down the stairs.

Chapter Nineteen

I loved him. I loved *them*. I don't know how it happened so quickly, but I knew in my heart that I loved all three of them.

Sitting on the cold concrete floor in scrubs that were made for a man, probably the same doctor who had delivered me eighteen years ago, suddenly all the stupid shit didn't seem so important anymore. What mattered was that I hadn't even gotten to say 'I love you' to the three men who had swooped in and captured my heart.

I didn't want to sleep for fear of passing out so hard that I might not hear anything upstairs. I could occasionally hear voices, but since Paul and Asher there had been no one.

I was losing my battle, fighting to keep my eyes open when I heard the lock slide in the door. It didn't open. I stood from my place on the floor, my ass stinging with pain from sitting in one place for so long. I wished I had shoes, but they were nowhere to be seen. I opened the metal door and crept up the stairs towards the door, listening intently.

Turn right. Run.

I played his words over and over in my head as I waited for chaos to erupt outside the door. I don't know what I expected, but it wasn't to hear gunfire erupt suddenly. I nearly fell but managed to hold onto the door handle to regain my balance.

Turn right. Run.

No matter what.

Turn right.

Run.

I took a deep breath, the tears already pouring down my cheeks like hot reminders that this wasn't a movie. This was real. I opened the door and tried not to look at what was ahead of me, because I was supposed to turn right and run.

Cages. Rows and rows of cages with angels. Turn right. Run.

My eyes scanned the sea of cages and Olly's bloodshot blue eyes met mine. I couldn't hear over all the noise but one word came from his mouth. *Run.*

I snapped my head to the right and took off, staying close to the wall. The gunfire was behind me now. My feet hurt from unknown debris digging into them, but I ran. There was a metal door straight ahead.

"Stop her!" Boots pounded on the cement behind me as I flung open the door and ran into the night.

The lights were on outside, the sky a deep blue color. My eyes scanned quickly, trying to figure out where I was supposed to go. Where I could hide. To my left was dark water, glittering in the artificial lights. Straight ahead were rows and rows of metal shipping containers with cranes towering over them, ready to put them on ships. To the right was chain link fencing, and beyond that, another building.

Hide. I needed to hide.

I ran as fast as I could and darted between the first two containers. The containers were arranged in groups of two with two groups in each row. They were stacked four containers high. The spaces between were narrow. I went towards the water and ran straight along the small strip of concrete between the containers and water. I would jump in if I needed to.

My lungs burned and I felt my airway not wanting to cooperate. I slowed slightly until I heard gunshots and shouts.

Where was I supposed to go? He said run. Run, run, run. That was what I did but now I was reaching the end of the area I was in and would run straight into the water. I turned at the last row, the chain link fence now in front of me. It went straight to the edge where the port met the water, but maybe I could hold onto the pole and slip around it? I definitely couldn't climb it since there was barbed wire at the top.

I ran towards the fence and slipped around the edge of it before stopping in my tracks. A black SUV was idling outside the building I was just in, and two large men were ushering a woman wearing a scarf around her head and sunglasses into the backseat. Before she climbed in she looked over at me.

"Danica! Run!" I heard Asher's yell, but didn't see him. I ran; there was not much cover between the fence and the next building over.

The sounds of boots on the pavement behind me was a reminder that I was being chased. A bullet hit the ground next to me and in a panic I lost my footing and fell onto the cement, my hands and knees scraping along the rough surface. I scrambled, trying to get up, to get farther away from the men, the bullets, the noise.

I managed to get up, but then was knocked back by a body tackling me, bullets hitting the ground, a scream of pain. Shouts. Curses. I struggled under the weight, the feel of warm blood seeping into the blue scrubs.

The body rolled over, the person gasping for air. I rose to my knees to run.

No.

The scream left my throat with so much force that I fell back, the world going silent around me before rushing back into my ears all at once.

No.

There was so much blood I didn't know where to put my hands to stop the flow of it. I pushed his blond hair out of his eyes and he stared back at me with sad slate blue eyes. Two blinks. A tear slid down his cheek.

No.

The gunfire had stopped. No more pounding feet. No more shouts. A ship's horn blew in the distance. The lulling sound of water filled my ears.

I put my lips against Asher's, his breath shuddering against them as I kissed him. "I love you, Asher." His hand gripped mine. He tried to speak but all that came from his mouth were gurgles.

Footsteps beside me. Silence.

Dad. He kneeled on the other side of Asher, his glowing hands hovering over his torso. He shook his head.

My sobs filled the night, the stars just making their appearance as Asher took a ragged breath. Seconds turned into minutes. No more breaths.

"Danica... they have to take him. They're being summoned."

I looked up at my father. He hadn't left his spot, but glanced to the side. I looked. Tobias. Olly. Tear-stained faces. Wings extended. Glazed eyes.

"They can't control it. They have to take him."

No.

Tobias walked forward, his wings folding back, but not away, and he scooped Asher in his arms. He backed away and they shot into the sky. Shooting stars.

Chapter Twenty

$\mathcal{D}$ad took me home and said he was staying a while, taking a vacation. Last time I checked, moping around on the couch with your daughter was not much of a vacation. He said that he left three of his most trusted demons in charge. I couldn't tell if he was serious or joking since he wasn't one to joke around.

It was the first time in recent memory where he stuck around longer than a day. The first time *ever*, at least that I could remember, that I had seen him out of a suit. He was a man who would arrive in a suit, go into the bedroom at night in a suit, and then come down the next morning in a suit. I guess it was just his way of expressing himself and showing he was in charge.

It was also the first time he watched more than the news and business channel. He binged on Netflix to humor his broken-hearted daughter.

"I find it rather peculiar that this Lucifer not only wears a suit constantly, but bears a striking resemblance to me. I'm going to have to figure out who is involved in making this show," he said, taking a bite out of a slice of pizza. I had talked him into watching *Lucifer*, curious to see his reaction. "I bet a dream demon planted that in someone's head."

I picked a piece of sausage off my plate and popped it in my mouth. I held myself back from shoving the entire extra-large pizza we had ordered into my face and devouring it like a pig. My appetite had been non-existent the last few days, but now it greeted me like a greedy child who wanted to take all the Halloween candy in the bowl.

"Do you think they're coming back?" I asked absently as I ate my crust, leaving the rest of the pizza. I had this thing with my pizza; I liked to eat my least favorite parts first, starting with the crust and ending with a small pile of sausage I picked off beforehand.

I had asked my father countless questions over the past few days, including what I was asking him now. Sometimes he didn't know the answer, sometimes he did. He would slip away into his office he never used, and talk on the phone to whoever was on the other end. Sometimes his answers would change the next time I circled back to them.

He put his plate on the coffee table and turned towards me. I focused on my pizza, folding it and biting into it. I probably shouldn't have been asking questions I didn't want the answers to while I was eating, but it was hard to resist. I needed to know, and if that meant crying into my pizza, then so be it.

"Ham says they are but there isn't a timeline. He doesn't know what's going on. No one does."

I met my father's eyes; he was serious. I let out a shaky breath and continued to eat. His answer meant it could be days, weeks, months, maybe even years. It had been three days since Tobias and Oliver had flown off into the night with Asher's lifeless body. Three days of radio silence from them and three days where I peppered my father with so many questions he probably wished he would have spent more years in my youth explaining celestial life to me.

The first day, I learned that the soul could only be restored once. Fallen that died, died for good. The second day, I learned that when an angel was summoned to heaven like Tobias and Olly were, that it was forced in dire circumstances, which is why they had glazed-over eyes. At least the third day brought me a little peace of mind, but just barely. They'd be back at some point. Tobias and Olly.

"Do you think they'll be Fallen?" I asked casually, like it wasn't a big deal. It was a very big deal. Olly might still have his mental state intact after, but Tobias would remember his death.

"Why would they be Fallen? They did nothing

wrong." He gave me a serious look, a concerned look. A look you give your child when they say something outlandish.

I shrugged, trying to show him I wasn't certain in my answer. "Because of me."

His face softened, a look I wasn't used to seeing often. Especially not with sweatpants and a t-shirt on. He almost looked like a normal dad. Almost.

"Love is not damning, Danica. It lightens the soul, puts it at ease, destroys the darkness. The souls that end up in hell, they don't love. They destroy it in themselves and those around them. Those that fall, fall because they hate more than they love. I fell because I hated more than loved." He paused and squeezed the bridge of his nose. "But love... love for you and for your mother..." His voice cracked as if he was holding back tears. "That love is what let me be free again."

"Does that mean your devil days are over?"

He chuckled and grabbed another slice of pizza, his emotions now tucked tightly away. I wish I could fold up my emotions and tuck them away just as easily.

"No. I am still going to run hell, at least for now, until this threat of opening another gate to hell is gone. I will be delegating a little more, something I should have done a long time ago."

"I don't understand how someone can open a gate to hell when you're right there."

"I only take up a small portion of hell. Heaven

and hell both run in infinitely expanding planes of existence. If someone decided to just keep walking straight in heaven or hell they will never find an end, it will continue to expand. There are some demons not under my control but they have always kept to themselves. My blood is the only key to hell so I don't know what they expect to do with all that angel blood they collected. I don't think it can create a gate by itself."

That was what worried me the most. None of us knew what their endgame was.

I HADN'T REALIZED how much I had missed Ava until she was lying next to me on my queen-sized bed. I had to tell her something about what had happened, but also couldn't tell her everything. She thought I was at an academy for troubled youth and we were being trained to go into the military. That was completely plausible given my track record and my dad's fortune. He could afford to send me to a top-secret military academy.

The reason for my tears was a little more difficult to explain. When I told her I had three boyfriends, she blinked at me for at least a minute, running it through her head. She was fairly innocent, only having made-out with a boyfriend, so the fact that I was with them all was a shocker for her. An even bigger shocker was that my dad didn't have anything bad to say about three men being in my life. I couldn't explain to her that he had been around so long that me having a harem of men wouldn't faze him. In fact, I think he was happy I had men around to protect me.

Well, now two men. Or maybe none if heaven didn't send them back to me.

"Are you sure you want to go back to that school? It sounds like torture. You should punch those bitches."

"I'm not doing too horribly in the classes. Mostly Cs. Plus, they might get out soon." I had told Ava that Olly and Tobias were taken by the court-martial since it was a military matter and I didn't know when or if they would come back.

I had decided that I couldn't just stay here and mope for the rest of my life. It had been almost a week. I could very well have moped back at school, where at least I'd have something to do to keep my mind off the overwhelming pain I felt inside.

Loud voices, one being my father, came from downstairs and we both sat up and looked at each other. Ava was up and out the door before I could stop her. It was so out of character for her that I quickly ran after her and grabbed her arm at the top of the stairs.

"You can't go down there! What are you doing?" I whisper shouted, yanking on her arm like it was the pull to a lawnmower. My dad had told me to stay upstairs with Ava until he came and got us.

"That voice..." she said on a sigh, still trying to descend down the steps.

I couldn't hear what the other voice was saying but it had a very seductive quality to it, like fine wine and dark chocolate if they could talk. I was certain it belonged to a demon, because why else would my best friend be in some kind of weird lust-filled trance trying to run to it.

The voices cut off and there was silence, except for Ava's deep breathing. She managed to snake her arm away and took the steps two at a time, holding onto the banister. Fuck my life, I couldn't even keep my best friend from throwing herself in harm's way.

I ran after her and collided into her back at the bottom of the stairs, nearly knocking her over. She was openly ogling a very attractive man who was leaning with his hip propped against the kitchen island. His skin was very tan, military shaved dark hair, and the most striking green eyes I had ever seen.

"Ricky, you didn't tell me you kept humans here. I would have turned it off had I known," he said, his eyes locked on Ava before glancing at me and then settling back on Ava. "I didn't take you for someone who has pets."

"I don't," Lucifer said, a slight tremor in his voice that probably only I could detect. Crap, this was bad. Why was there even a demon in our house?

"And I certainly didn't know you liked them so young."

"Well, I definitely can't have prostitutes that have been used. Ladies, why don't you head back upstairs? I was just about done." He stepped in between us and gave me a very serious look that told me to go with it.

Ava shook her head and looked back and forth between me and him. I grabbed her arm and yanked her back upstairs before she could get a word out.

"You're no fun, Ricky." I could almost imagine the pout on the man's face. It sounded like he was throwing out his bottom lip.

"Stop calling me that."

"Fine, you're no fun, *Lucy*."

I heard a smack and a laugh as I shut my door and leaned up against it. Ava slowly sank on the bed, still seeming out of it. I had no clue what kind of demon that was but I was certain it couldn't be anything good.

"Are you okay?" I stayed in front of the door, not sure if she was going to take off out of it again.

She put her hand over her heart and took several deep breaths. I could see her trembling from my spot against the door. She met my eyes and a huge smile spread across her face. Oh, no. I knew that face. That was the same face she made when her beloved Nick Jonas came on the screen or radio.

"I know this is crazy, but I think I'm in love with that man." She stood and went to the window.

Shit, was she going to climb out the window now? I rushed over to her and grabbed her biceps. I sighed in relief when all she did was pull the curtains back and stare outside into the darkness. Although, maybe that should have concerned me even more.

"What did he do to you?" I still kept my hand on her arm and she turned her head to look at me.

"Stole my heart, that's what he did."

I MANAGED to convince Ava that she had been dreaming and that my dad never had business associates over to the house or anyone else for that matter. Crisis averted.

I decided it was time to attempt to get back to school. I was already behind, but surprisingly not as far behind as I was in human school. Everyone at school knew what happened and instead of looking at me like I would murder them, they looked at me with indifference and maybe a touch of curiosity.

Rumors of my scream had spread fast since several third-year students were part of the rescue mission. When I screamed with everything that was in my heart and soul, something had happened. Something that I had already tried to replicate countless times once my dad finally spilled the beans about it. At the time it happened, I hadn't even noticed because I was so distraught.

But when I had screamed, the Fallen dropped to their knees and dropped their weapons. It made no sense to me. It made no sense to anyone. The Fallen hadn't even known what had come over them, but described it as a compulsion to surrender.

We learned nothing more than we already knew from the Fallen. Someone wanted to open a gate to hell and needed angel blood to do it. My role in it all was still unclear. Maybe I was the sacrificial lamb or leverage. All we knew was that the mystery woman and John Adamson Sr. were nowhere to be found. John Jr. was back at school; apparently the charges against him and his father for drug trafficking, distribution, and coercion were dropped.

I spent my nights off campus at Asher's place because I needed to be close to him, to them, and the only place I felt that way was in his bed or on his roof. Since the weather was getting a smidgen warmer, I'd pull his duvet off his bed and sleep on a reclining lounge chair under the stars.

The stars, the moon, the faint sounds of revelers down the street always relaxed me enough to fall asleep, even though sleep was painful. The scene played on repeat night after night. Me turning right and running, running, running. Until Asher threw himself on me and died.

My nightmares seemed to suddenly stop and I could finally get decent sleep. In fact, I found myself looking forward to sleeping every night, where I'd get lost in a dream so vivid and enjoyable that it made me feel guilty considering Tobias and Oliver were still missing.

Two weeks had passed since returning to school, three since my world imploded. It was early for me to sleep, barely nine, but I'd had a long day dealing with the sneers and under-their-breath comments from the Divine 7. They had been so quiet that it surprised and saddened me to hear their demeaning remarks yet again.

To make the day worse, now Spring had decided to bring a shower with it, the sprinkles hitting the duvet I had just gotten comfortable under. I grumbled curses at the sky and trudged my way to the door, the duvet trailing after me.

"Danica?" My hand was on the door knob and I froze at the sound of my name on Tobias's lips. My heart sped up and I dropped the duvet as I turned around.

Tobias and Oliver stood in the middle of the roof, their wings still extended. They were dressed in white cotton pants, no shoes. I stepped forward, over the duvet. Was I dreaming?

They both turned their heads and looked at each other and their wings folded back and away. My heart stopped and I reached out and grabbed onto the back of the chair near me.

Asher.

His eyes met mine and a grin spread across his

face as he moved his wings in the smallest of movements. I couldn't move, the shock and awe too much. Olly and Tobias passed by me, hugging me tightly, but my eyes stayed glued to Asher. They laughed and went inside, leaving me on the roof with him.

"Are you going to fuckin' stand there and stare or come here?"

"Are angels allowed to cuss like that?" I finally regained my composure and met him halfway.

He brought his hand to my cheek and wiped away the tears that I hadn't even felt falling with the raindrops that were hitting my face. Then he pulled me into him, wrapping his arms and wings around me.

"I'm sorry we couldn't come back sooner. They had to go find my soul," he said as if it was the most normal thing in the world to have his buddies go track down his lost soul. "Let's get inside."

It was an out of body experience being reunited with my angels. I had almost come to terms with the fact that not even the two I thought were alive were coming back.

Shock. That's what I felt. After spending weeks in a steady state of grief that had numbed me, the onslaught of feelings ripped my heart out of my chest, put it in a blender, then shoved it all back in my chest cavity creating a gooey mess.

We sat on the couch, draped over each other like a pile of puppies. There was so much I wanted to say, so much I needed to know. They had been gone for practically a month and it had felt like an essential part of me was missing.

"Asher is the first of his kind. Never has a soul been plucked out of the pit of lost souls," Olly explained, stuffing a cookie in his mouth. In heaven, the need for food was nonexistent so he was eating enough cookies to make up for the lost time.

"How? Why?"

"Angel baby and Toby went to the outskirts of heaven where the lost souls are sent. It's kind of like a prison but the souls just float around like jellyfish in the ocean, can't communicate, no corporeal form, just there in solitude and silence. Probably a couple of weeks passed and I felt them getting closer but I couldn't yell for them. The next thing I know, they were standing buck naked in front of my soul. I'd never been so happy to see two limp dicks before in my life." Asher twirled my hair around his finger as he spoke.

"Why were you naked" I asked Olly and Tobias.

"Couldn't risk a soul getting their hands on something they can attach to," Tobias explained. "A soul by itself can't escape that part of heaven, but if it attaches itself to an item it can."

"So they got me out and here I am. My job wasn't done yet." Asher looked at Tobias and Olly and they nodded before he continued. "There is a prophecy that was delivered to Michael by Nostradamus that when the darkness overshadowed the light, a baby would be born to the creator's two greatest regrets. That baby would grow into a woman and save the light from the dark with her four guardians."

"When did the darkness overshadow the light?" My heart was beating wildly in my chest, knowing what they were going to tell me. Why else would they be telling me about some prophecy from Nostradamus? I was always under the impression that Nostradamus was a quack job who just had a way with words that could fit multiple situations.

"January 20, 2001."

My birthday. I shut my eyes and took a deep breath. *Crap.* That was a lot to take in. "It makes sense Lucifer was a regret, but my mother? She was just a human who ran a coffee shop." I watched as the three faces around me fell into contemplative frowns. "Right?"

Suddenly, I wasn't so sure, unless the human race was a regret. That would be much more depressing than finding out I was half swamp creature or something. I opened my eyes and Olly took my hand, rubbing his thumb in small circles in the palm. I felt myself relax slightly but not nearly enough to stop the slight panic welling up inside of me. My mom *had* to be a human. She had to be.

"Your mom is Lilith."

Epilogue

Reve

One week ago

*S*he was curled up on the rooftop chair again, a blanket covering her, her brown hair fanning around her face and shoulders. She was a fragile-looking thing. If I dropped her she would shatter into shards that would pierce the skin deep. Striking. Deadly. Beautiful.

I wanted her shards to pierce me.

I ignored my other assignments and decided to take this detour; one night would not set me back in my work. Besides, the bossman was surprisingly distracted and he would never know. He'd never know that I was about to do something that was forbidden. Something based on a feeling that I'm not even capable of.

Her cries were just too tempting to ignore. She was vulnerable. Broken. Delectable. I needed a taste of her.

I descended and landed in a crouch at the foot of the chair. No one was ever up there with her, she was always alone. It was just her and her sorrows that filled the night with her cries for what she'd lost. I wanted to feel her pain as badly as a root wants to touch water during a drought.

My body hovered over hers, my breath causing a single strand of her hair to move. I wanted to take her hair in my hands and let it cascade between my fingers like a waterfall. I traced my finger along her jawline, not touching the skin. I wondered what her skin might feel like under my fingertips. Would I taint it with my touch?

I stifled back a groan. I shouldn't have been doing this. I should have been down the street giving Mr. Campbell the nightmare he deserved. But I was too close now. I shut my eyes and pushed my way into her dream.

SHE WAS RUNNING, gunshots all around. Feet pounding the pavement behind her.

She was tackled, shielded by a man's body, who took the gunshots aimed at her.

She screamed.

An endless cycle of pain.

She was running, gunshots all around. Feet pounding the pavement behind her.

I grabbed her and took off into the night.

I SHOULDN'T HAVE DONE it. I should have left her there in her misery and feasted on it. I am the bringer of nightmares, not an eradicator of terrors. If anything, I should have made it worse by having all of the men she loved fall to their deaths.

Her scream was what did it. I had heard my fair share of screams, usually feasting on the fear and pain in them, fueling myself. Her scream made my skin crawl and my heart sputter like it was running out of fuel.

So I grabbed her and plopped her into a new dream.

SHE WAS GORGEOUS, standing at the top of the wide staircase, her hair in loose curls around her face. Her dress was red with a lace-up corset bodice and mermaid bottom. My choice. She smoothed her hands down her hips, unsure of herself. She was a princess tonight; my princess.

Eyes were drawn to her and a blush creeped up to her cheeks, turning them slightly pink. She slowly made her way down the steps in her heels, which were probably an inch too high for her. I'd remember to make them shorter next time I put her in heels. Three inches instead of four.

She reached the bottom of the staircase and moved into the crowd. I let her have some control of the dream, but still held the strings tightly in my grasp. A group of three approached her, two young women and a young man. They greeted her with hugs and laughter.

I watched from afar, taking her in. Her smile. Her lips. The curve of her shoulders. My mouth watered for the taste of her, the smile on her lips, the feeling of her skin against mine.

If this was a nightmare I would have killed her three friends right then and there. I would have made her watch as I peeled back their skin. I would have feasted on her screams.

I walked towards her, tipping my head back to drink the last of my champagne. It went down smoothly. I passed a server and put the flute on the silver tray. I adjusted my cuff links and straightened my bow tie.

She was only a few feet away. I approached, touching her elbow gently, the touch sending a jolt through my body like a lightning bolt.

She turned towards me, her eyebrows raised in curiosity, a smile still on her face. She didn't pull her arm away and I didn't pull my hand away.

Nothing Else Matters *by Metallica began playing as couples took to the large dance floor under the sparkling chandeliers to waltz.*

I bent at the waist, keeping my eyes locked on hers, and offered her my hand. "May I have this dance?"

Also by Maya Nicole

Celestial Academy

Ascend

Descend

Transcend

Standalones

Widow

Infernal Council

Infuse

Made in the USA
Monee, IL
13 July 2020

36413614R10174